BLOTTO, TW1
BOOTLEGC

BLOTTO, TWINKS AND THE BOOTLEGGER'S MOLL

Simon Brett

WINDSOR
PARAGON

First published 2012
by Constable,
an imprint of Constable & Robinson Ltd
This Large Print edition published 2013
by AudioGO Ltd
by arrangement with
Constable & Robinson

Hardcover   ISBN: 978 1 4713 2332 4
Softcover   ISBN: 978 1 4713 2333 1

British Library Cataloguing in Publication Data available

Printed and bound in Great Britain by
MPG Books Group Limited

*To Alastair and Sarah,
with congratulations on their wedding*

1

A Bit of a Wet Blanket

Tawcester Towers, though a magnificent stately home in many respects, had always rather fallen down on its plumbing. Houseguests, usually arriving in the comforting expectation of a murder being committed and solved by a conveniently present polymathic amateur sleuth within the weekend, had to get used to strange nocturnal noises reverberating through the ancient structure. And though some of these noises could be put down to brandy-steeped fellow guests up to no good with chambermaids in the servants' quarters, most of them were entirely attributable to the plumbing.

The house's superannuated lead pipes were capable of a range of sounds which would put the average church organ to shame. Baths filling set up an ominous irregular clanking, similar to that made by a small contingent of sabre-rattling hussars. Baths emptying gave a passable impression of Chinamen being strangled by their own pigtails in Limehouse opium dens. While any guest incautious enough to flush one of the few water closets in the middle of the night would unleash a cacophony of coughing, gasping and spluttering that would not have sounded out of place in the advanced ward of a tuberculosis sanatorium.

And when, at four in the morning, some unfortunate skivvy fired up the Tawcester Towers boiler to heat water that would be cold again by the time it reached the house's furthest bathrooms, the pipes set up a creaking, wheezing and gurgling that was indistinguishable from the laugh of the Dowager Duchess of Tawcester.

Very few of the houseguests, however, would be aware of the similarity, because the sound of the Dowager Duchess laughing was as rare in Tawcester Towers as the mating call of the Peruvian Booby. There were not many things in life she found amusing, except for patronizing servants and insulting people of her own rank. The heavily powdered immemorial granite from which her features had been carved rarely allowed its surface to be cracked by a smile.

Her younger son, the Honourable Devereux Lyminster, universally known to his equals as 'Blotto', was of a considerably cheerier disposition. Every morning when his manservant Tweedling drew back his bedroom curtains, the beams of the sun were met by an answering beam on Blotto's impossibly handsome face. Its features were never clouded by a dark thought . . . and indeed rarely by a thought of any kind.

When the Almighty—or whoever organizes these things—created Blotto, He was somewhat parsimonious in His allocation of brains. But given all the other gifts the young man had been granted—birth into one of the foremost aristocratic families in the land, breathsapping good looks, exceptional skills at whichever sport he turned his hand to, and instinctive, unthinking bravery in the face of any danger—his deficiency in the brain department never bothered anyone. It certainly never bothered Blotto himself.

Besides, he had a sister whose abilities more than compensated for his own intellectual shortcomings.

Lady Honoria Lyminster, universally known to her equals as 'Twinks', was as beautiful as her brother was handsome, and as brilliant as he was thick. It was a constant amazement to Blotto that her delicate head, under its bob of silky blonde hair, could generate so much brainpower. He could only think that his sister's cranium was like one of those structures read of in fairy stories, whose interior is infinitely bigger than logic dictates is possible.

One sunny summer morning Blotto woke in the customary manner, to the clatter of curtain rings as Tweedling vouchsafed admission to the day. 'Good morning, Tweedling,' he mumbled.

'Good morning, milord.'

This exchange was always the full extent of their matitudinal conversation. Though Blotto invariably woke in sunny mood, he was not at his most talkative first thing in the morning, a fact that Tweedling recognized and accepted. Had the young master wished to volunteer more words, the manservant would undoubtedly have responded to them, but that rarely happened. Tweedling's unvarying morning ritual was to knock on Blotto's bedroom door, enter without waiting for permission, draw back the curtains, exchange the above greetings, place the tea tray on the bedside table and exit sharply.

Some young men, Blotto knew, had deeper relationships with their manservants. They might discuss horse-racing tips, the prospects for the day's hunting, the bizarre behaviours of houseguests, or the peccadillos of actresses. Blotto never had conversations of that kind with Tweedling. He regarded the manservant simply as a convenience in his life, a functional implement, perhaps slightly

3

more versatile than a knife, fork or spoon, but otherwise not dissimilar.

That particular morning, as consciousness trickled back into the veins of his splendid frame, Blotto was aware of something rather unusual. His bedding was distinctly wet.

Now, he was used to damp sheets. They were a feature of bedrooms in English public schools and stately homes. Even at the height of summer a slight musty clamminess clung to all baronial bedding. It was one of those quintessential features of English life, like cold draughts and warm beer, which were expected and accepted by everyone except for mollycoddled Americans.

But Blotto's bed that morning was suffering from more than a bracing dampness. His bolster, sheets, blankets and counterpane were all wringing wet.

The wheels within Blotto's brain clicked round slowly as he tried to produce an explanation for this phenomenon. He reassembled his recollections of the previous night, aware of the accidents that could be caused by alcoholic excess. But no, his conscience was clear on that score. His intake had been very modest—three or four scotch and sodas before dinner, a couple of bottles of claret with the meal, and then maybe half a dozen large brandies in the billiard room by way of *digestifs*. Nothing out of the ordinary, and certainly nothing to overstrain the bladder of a healthy young man like Blotto.

Seeking another solution, he looked up towards the ceiling. He wasn't aware of there having been torrential rain during the night, nor indeed of a hurricane tearing off the roof of Tawcester Towers, but he knew himself to be a heavy sleeper, so he supposed such eventualities were possible.

4

And looking upwards did reveal, if not an explanation of the inundation, then at least its source. The ceiling was sagging and bellied out and, from a large tear in its fabric, water still dripped.

While he was still lying in his soggy sheets, taking in the extent of the damage, there was a sharp rat-a-tat on his door and, with a cry of 'Hope you're decent, me old bloater!', Twinks burst into the room.

Blotto never tired of looking at his sister. As an entrant in the Pulchritude Stakes, her Starting Price would be at least a hundred to one on. She really was the lark's larynx. In fact she was as beautiful as he was handsome, though of course Blotto never gave his own looks a second thought. It didn't do for chaps to be aware of that kind of guff, not healthy. That was the sort of thing foreigner boddos did, like boasting about being good at cricket (not, of course, that they would have been good at cricket, because they were foreign).

That Twinks still looked beautiful that morning was no thanks to her couture. She wore Wellington boots and a man's trench-coat. Her blonde bob was obscured by a yellow oilskin sou'wester. The only article of her more usual ensemble was the sequinned reticule that dangled from her slender wrist. Water dripped off her, puddling on the wooden boards of the bedroom floor.

She grinned cheerily at her soggy brother. 'Looks like we're in the same boat, me old biscuit barrel. Or actually it looks more like the boat we're both in has capsized.'

'It's a bit of a chock in the cogwheel, isn't it?' said Blotto, whose brain had not yet quite lumbered into wakefulness. He looked up at the dripping hole above. 'What's the bizz-buzz on this, Twinks? Is it one of those forty-days-and-forty-nights raining jobs like the one that happened to that poor old pineapple in the Bible whose name escapes me? Should we start pairing up animals and collecting gopher wood to build an ark? Though I'm not sure where the nearest supplier of gopher wood is . . . or indeed what gopher wood is . . . Oh, broken biscuits, what is the name of the boddo I'm talking about?'

'Noah.'

'Of course. You're bong on the nose there, Twinks.'

'Anyway, Blotto me old tin tray, this is no job for Noah. What we're up against here isn't a natural disaster.'

'Not of the raining for forty days and forty nights and pairing up animals kind?'

'Absolutely not. The gluepot we're currently in is entirely man-made. The plumbing system of Tawcester Towers has finally had enough. It's given in its notice!'

'So where's all the spoffing water come from, by Denzil?' asked Blotto. Plumbing was one of the many areas of life on which his information was a bit sketchy. It certainly hadn't been on the curriculum when he'd been at Eton. Mind you, there were many subjects that had been on the curriculum there about which his knowledge was equally sketchy. Blotto's brain wasn't good at retaining information unrelated to hunting or cricket.

Twinks of course was just as skilled in plumbing as she was in everything else. In fact at that moment her dainty reticule contained a set of

spanners, pipe-cutting and -bending tools, along
with a tin of Plumber's Mait, which would be equal
to most minor repairs. But she had already deduced
that the Tawcester Towers disaster would need
professional assistance.

'The water,' she informed her brother, 'that is
currently drenching us comes from the tanks in the
lofts at the top of the building. It is they that supply
all of our domestic water.'

Blotto nodded thoughtfully. Not being given
to abstruse philosophical enquiry, he had never
thought to enquire as to where water came from.
So far as he was concerned, you just turned on a tap
and there it was. Rather like money, in that respect.

'So this water that is currently drenching us,' he
said slowly, 'has come through the lofts . . . through
the floor above us and—'

'Great whistling wallabies!' his sister interrupted.

'What's up, Twinks?'

'"The floor above us"! You know what's on the
floor above us, don't you, Blotters?'

'Water?' he hazarded.

'The Long Gallery!' cried Twinks, as she rushed
for the door. 'The Long Gallery containing all of
the family portraits!'

*   *   *

It was as she had feared. Water had soaked the
portraits of all the Dukes of Tawcester (including
the Gainsborough and Reynolds, which had been
stolen by a criminal mastermind called La Puce
and reclaimed by Blotto and Twinks in the face of
many terrible dangers). Those two had depicted
Rupert the Smug and Rupert the Incapable. (All

of the Dukes of Tawcester had been called Rupert, and many had gathered suitable adjectives to their name, like Black Rupert and Rupert the Dull.)

Brother and sister looked across the Long Gallery in despair. The water had stained and discoloured the paintings, causing the ancient canvases to sag, balloon and tear. This irreplaceable record of Tawcester family history lay in tatters.

'Well, that's a bit of a candle-snuffer,' said Blotto.

2

A Summons to the Blue Morning Room

Practical affairs inside Tawcester Towers which concerned the wellbeing of the house's residents and guests were organized by the butler Grimshaw and his limitless cohorts of housekeepers, cooks, footmen, maids of various grades, bootboys and other domestics too insignificant to be given titles.

Practical affairs outside Tawcester Towers were dealt with by an army of gardeners, grooms, farmhands, chauffeurs and an assortment of semi-literate yokels, under the iron hand of the Estate Manager, Mr McEnemy. He was a Scotsman of implacable pessimism, whose dourness could scour out from any cloud the last vestige of a silver lining. Since his duties also extended to maintenance of the fabric of Tawcester Towers, he was quickly summoned to assess the damage caused by the plumbing disaster.

As the Estate Manager moved from room to

room his face lengthened and the note of grim satisfaction in his voice deepened. He was prone to Presbyterian visions of apocalyptic disasters, of fire, brimstone and floods of biblical proportions. A man who lived in perpetual anticipation of doom could not fail to be heartened by such a complete confirmation of his worst presentiments that the tour of Tawcester Towers' interior offered that morning.

Blotto and Twinks accompanied him. Dealing with the Estate Manager was too lowly a task to come within the remit of their older brother. The current Duke of Tawcester, universally known to his equals as 'Loofah', did not deal with the minutiae of life. In fact, one would be hard put to think of anything he did deal with. Apart for his annual visit to the House of Lords on the day when they did an excellent Christmas lunch, Loofah's main task in life was impregnating his wife the Duchess, universally known to her equals as 'Sloggo', with a child that wasn't another girl. The male Tawcester line had to be continued, or else the dukedom would devolve to Loofah's younger brother—and even Blotto himself recognized what a disaster that would be. It was not a role that he coveted. In fact he didn't covet any role that might interrupt his priorities of hunting, cricket and a little light sleuthing.

As they came to the end of their tour of inspection, Mr McEnemy's face was as long as that of a horse which had just been pipped at the post in the Grand National. 'This,' he pronounced with morbid glee, 'is too big a job for any of my staff. I have handymen who can replace a ballcock or fit a new washer to a dripping tap, but work on this

9

scale is beyond them. The entire plumbing system of Tawcester Towers will need to be replaced, root and branch.'

'Surely you'd use pipes?' said Blotto.

'I dinna ken what you mean, milord.'

'Well, replacing the pipes with roots and branches would be—'

'I think Mr McEnemy was speaking metaphorically,' said Twinks gently.

'Ah.' Her brother nodded his head, giving a very good—though misleading—impression of someone who knew what 'metaphorically' meant.

'This is a job,' Mr McEnemy announced, 'that is going to cost thoosands and thoosands of poonds. And that's before ye start to think of the restoration work on the paintings.' He rubbed his hands together in gleeful despair.

* * *

From the nursery onwards a summons by their mother to the Blue Morning Room had had ominous connotations for Blotto and Twinks. They always knew they had committed some serious violation of the cast-iron code by which the Dowager Duchess ensured that everything was conducted in Tawcester Towers. Their misdemeanour, they recognized, must have been a serious one . . . perhaps using the billiard room's lights for target practice with one of the Duke's shotguns . . . or playing hunting games in the Long Gallery on real horses . . . or talking about money . . . or even the cardinal sin of being pleasant to a member of the domestic staff. Any one of these and a million other peccadillos could bring down the

10

wrath of the Dowager Duchess.

Her means of punishment was never corporal. She was confident that her offspring would receive the requisite amount of beating from nannies and governesses, and later from the nuns at Twinks's convent and, for Blotto, the beaks at Eton. No, the Dowager Duchess's disciplinary action was always verbal, but not a whit the less painful for that. The ability to diminish her inferiors and insult her equals had been passed down through the generations, and refined to new levels of viciousness with each one. The idea that she might temper this ingrained malignancy when dealing with her own children would have appalled her as much as the idea of cuddling them.

There were gradations in the Dowager Duchess's verbal punishments, but the direst—the one that would have had the infant Blotto shaking in his silk knee-breeches—was the admission that she was 'disappointed' in her son's behaviour.

Blotto and Twinks knew therefore what they were in for when, that day in the Blue Morning Room, their mother, seated in a Chippendale chair which contrived to look like a throne, announced, 'I was very disappointed by what happened yesterday.'

Though no twisting of logic could attribute any blame to either of them for the state of the Tawcester Towers plumbing, both siblings felt an immediate pang of guilt. Their mother's manner could have made them feel personal responsibility for Noah's Flood, let alone the one in their own home.

'And,' the Dowager Duchess continued imperially, 'it has put the family in something of a fix.'

11

'In what way, Mater?' asked her son, who frequently liked to have things spelled out for him. 'I mean, yes, it's a stye in the eye having hot and cold running water on the walls, but there are boddos around who sort out that kind of rombooley ... you know, plumbers and so on. I think there are even pineapples out there who'll do you a patchwork and paint job on the family portraits. So as of this mo the situation's a bit of a candle-snuffer, but in no time it can be brought back to zing-zing condition. All that's required is that Mr McEnemy gets on the old ringbox to call up a couple of these boddos and the whole thing's creamy éclair.'

'Unfortunately, Blotto,' his mother rumbled, 'that is not all that's required. The stye in the eye is rather bigger than you have envisaged.'

'In what way, Mater?'

'There certainly are among the peasant classes artisans with the skills you enumerate, but there is one thing you do not seem to be taking into account.'

'And what's that?'

'All such people require payment.'

'Well, Mater, that's not such a tough rusk to chew. We simply pay them.'

'There is nothing simple about it, Blotto. Payment requires money.'

'Then that's the stuff to use,' advised Blotto wisely.

For a moment wordless, the Dowager Duchess growled, like a volcano having decided to give up being extinct, so Twinks interposed to explain the situation.

'The fact is, Blotto, that the mater always

12

brought us up to know that talking about money was vulgar . . .'

'Good ticket,' he agreed.

'. . . so, as a result, we never have talked about money . . .'

'I'm still on the same page, Twinks.'

'. . . but if you don't talk about money . . .'

'Which we don't, because it's vulgar.'

'Agreed. But if you don't talk about it . . .'

'Yes?'

'. . . then it's very difficult to know whether you've got any or not . . .'

'Ah.'

'. . . and the fact is that now . . . we haven't got any.'

The full impact of this finally got through to Blotto. 'Broken biscuits . . .' he murmured. Then, recovering, he said, 'But surely, when these boddos are dealing with people like us—you know, members of the aristocracy—surely they'd be snuffled up to do the job just for the honour of doing it?'

'Sadly not,' boomed the Dowager Duchess, her power of speech returned. 'There has been a great decline in standards in this country recently. Beating the Boche in the recent dust-up was not an unmitigated bonus. Apart from making it difficult to maintain cordial relations with family members who are German, it has also had a shocking effect on the morals of the British common man. The filthy doctrines of Socialism are discussed openly in the nation's high streets. As a result, tradespeople have become insolent, unwilling to extend credit even to the highest in the land.' A cloud crossed her craggy features. 'I was never entirely convinced,' she pronounced, 'that the ending of the feudal system was a step forward.'

The three of them shared a thoughtful silence, which was broken by a very excited Blotto. 'I've just had a real buzzbanger of an idea!'

'Oh?' There was a wealth of scepticism in the Dowager Duchess's monosyllable. Past experience had taught her not to get disproportionately excited about her younger son's 'buzzbangers'.

'I met a boddo once,' Blotto went on enthusiastically, 'whose castle burnt down. Some tweenie had dropped a fag-end in the kitchen, something like that. Whole place went up like a spoffing Roman candle. And, do you know, he got money to build the whole thing up again. Didn't use it for that, of course. Moved to the Riviera and spent the lot on tight spongers and loose women. Nice story, though—pure strawberry jam with dollops of cream.'

'But how did he get the money?' asked Twinks patiently.

'Ah. Right. With you.' Blotto grinned before unleashing his bombshell. 'From the insurance!'

He turned towards his mother, hopeful of commendation. The Dowager Duchess focused on her son a look that could have made a housemaid spontaneously combust at a hundred and fifty yards. 'Insurance?' she echoed, shrivelling the word to ashes with contempt. 'Insurance is the last refuge of the vulgarian!'

'But, Mater—'

'Why don't you ever listen to me, Blotto? I have already told you my views on the subject of insurance.'

'Oh, I'm sorry, Mater. When was—?'

14

'When the Gainsborough and the Reynolds were stolen from the Long Gallery! At the time you asked fatuously whether the paintings were insured, and I thought I made it clear to you then that insurance is a system devised by small-minded shopkeepers for small-minded shopkeepers. Besides, taking out insurance would involve letting members of the hoi polloi to invade here to ...' she shuddered at the awfulness of the notion '... to value the contents, as if Tawcester Towers were some kind of common pawnshop.'

Blotto deduced from his mother's words that she wasn't very keen on the idea of insurance.

'Oh, for the love of strawberries!' said his sister. 'There must be some way we can make money to pay for the repairs. 'Have you had a pow-wow with your man of business, Mater? Surely he can organize a mortgage for us?'

'I have spoken to my man of business,' the Dowager Duchess replied solemnly, 'and he informs me that Tawcester Towers is already mortgaged to the hilt. If not rather deeper.'

'Oh, that rather takes the icing off the Swiss bun, doesn't it?' said Twinks.

There was another gloomy silence. Then Blotto's face was suddenly suffused with red, his eyes sparkled and his hands curled into triumphant fists. His mother and sister both recognized the symptoms. Blotto was about to announce another buzzbanger of an idea.

And so indeed it proved. 'I've got it!' he cried. 'Got it as tight as a rabbit in a snare! I think you'll find I've come up with the silverware this time, Mater.'

'So what is your latest idea, Blotto?' asked his

mother without optimism. 'Are you prepared to share it with us?'

'I certainly am. And when you hear it, you'll be as chuffed as a cheetah who's just downed his first gazelle.' He paused for dramatic effect. Which was quite a brave thing to do. The Dowager Duchess wasn't very keen on pauses that she hadn't initiated. 'There's a thing I've heard of ... and I think it's quite popular ... and people get paid money to do it. So if I went out and got one of these things ... then I'd get paid for doing it ... and our troubles would be at an end.'

'Blotto,' demanded his mother. 'Are you suggesting that you should get a job?'

'You've hit it bong on the nose there, Mater!'

The way the Dowager Duchess's face empurpled to the colour of long-hung venison gave Blotto an inkling that she was less than enthusiastic about his idea.

And this impression was reinforced by her next speech. 'Blotto, did you not take in anything that you were taught during your upbringing?'

'Well, not much, no. I was never a whale on school work, you know that, and—'

'I am not referring to your lack of academic prowess. That couldn't matter less to a person of your breeding. I am referring to the values that I would have hoped growing up here at Tawcester Towers, under my tutelage and that of your late father the Duke, would have inculcated in you, values that should be second nature to people of our class.'

Blotto was having a bit of difficulty following her drift, but he didn't say anything as the Dowager Duchess stormed on, 'And yet now I hear you

16

brazenly suggesting, to my face, that you should work for a living! I am in a state of shock at the very idea! That a member of the Tawcester family should go out to work ... well, it's an appalling notion! I can hardly believe that I heard the words coming from your lips. If you were not supposedly now an adult, I would send you instantly from the room to wash your mouth out with soap and water. As it is, all I can say, Blotto, is that I am deeply *disappointed* in you.'

He recoiled as if struck in the face, but her words were far more hurtful than any physical blow could have been. 'I get the impression, M-mater,' he stuttered, 'that you don't think it's a good idea for me to go out and get a job.'

'I am glad,' the Dowager Duchess rumbled, 'that you have taken that point on board. Anyway, the reason I called you both here to the Blue Morning Room is that I have devised a solution to our current impecunity. It's not an attractive one—indeed, it's downright distasteful—but desperate times call for desperate measures.'

She launched her own dramatic pause, which was ended by Twinks asking, 'What is it, Mater?'

The Dowager Duchess drew herself up in her Chippendale throne, in the manner of a judge donning his black cap prior to passing a death sentence, before announcing, 'I am going to marry Blotto off to an American!'

3

Blotto's Fate Is Sealed

Blotto was appalled to discover how far his mother had already advanced with her salvage plan. She hadn't just come up with the general concept of marrying him off to an American, she had selected the actual American to whom he was to be married off.

The lucky girl's name, the Dowager Duchess informed her son, was Mary Chapstick. 'She is the daughter of Luther P. Chapstick III.'

'And who's he when he's got his spats on?' asked Blotto disconsolately.

'He is a meat-packing magnate.'

Her son looked confused. 'What, you mean he's got special powers to lift up cans of meat and—?'

'Not that kind of magnet.'

'I didn't know there was any other kind.'

'A magnate,' said the Dowager Duchess, shuddering with contempt at the very thought, 'is a commercially successful businessman in the manufacturing line.'

'Oh,' said Blotto.

'And while it would be unbelievably bad form for us to mix with that kind of person this side of the Atlantic, apparently such connections would not be frowned on at all in America. So when you're safely ensconced over there, there will be no question of our family honour being sullied.'

Blotto didn't like the direction that the conversation was taking. 'What exactly do you mean, Mater, by the expression "safely ensconced"?'

'I mean when you are married to Mary Chapstick.'

He was appalled. 'Are you suggesting that, when we're married, we won't live here?'

'Of course you won't, Blotto. It's the chit's money we're after, not her company.'

'But I'll be stuck with her company. And stuck with it in America of all places,' said Blotto pathetically. 'Won't you miss me?'

The Dowager Duchess gave a curious look to her son before replying, 'No. Of course not.' She didn't subscribe to any of this new-fangled nonsense about loving one's children. Or touching them . . . yeugh.

Suddenly she snorted like a water buffalo being teased by a horse-fly. 'Anyway, Blotto, living in America will be a small sacrifice for you to make in the cause of preserving the family honour . . . and of getting the Tawcester Towers plumbing replaced.'

*   *   *

'Well, it's a pretty big stye in the eye, let me tell you,' said Blotto miserably when, the audience with their mother over, the two siblings had retired to Twinks's boudoir. There she was busying herself making them restorative cups of cocoa. Using her own electric kettle, mixing the stuff herself, not ringing for a housemaid to do any of it! She really is a dashed modern girl, my sister, thought Blotto fondly.

But his love for Twinks was for once insufficient to lift his mood. He had always had an allergy to the idea of matrimony. The institution seemed to offer nothing except the guarantee that a boddo's freedom would be curtailed. Still, Blotto was sufficient of a realist to recognize that at some point inevitably a bachelor in his position would be traded in the matrimonial market. Thus far he had managed to thwart his mother's plans to marry him off, but he knew he'd be living in a fool's paradise to imagine that the state of affairs could continue for ever.

So it wasn't the thought of marriage that was clouding his sunny disposition as much as the idea of having to live away from his beloved Tawcester Towers. His demands in life were simple— adequate feeding and watering and, during the relevant seasons, unlimited amounts of hunting and cricket. The idyllic family estate offered, in Blotto's estimation, unrivalled facilities to meet these modest needs.

But the idea of living in America . . . a country where, according to rumours he had heard, most hunting involved the use of firearms and where they didn't even play cricket, and where their national sport was that girls' game, rounders . . . well, it really took the jam off the biscuit.

It never occurred to him to argue with his mother's diktat. The Dowager Duchess's knowledge of protocol was impeccable, and if she said that it would be too shaming for him to appear in English society with an American wife, then she must be right. So he would have to become reconciled to giving up the things he loved most, hunting and cricket. Oh, and Twinks of course, whom he loved dearly . . . though obviously not as much as hunting and cricket.

When she had handed him his cocoa and sat

down opposite, warming her delicate hands on the mug, Blotto looked hopefully into his sister's azure eyes. If anyone could come up with an escape route from his current swamphole, it had to be Twinks and her brilliant brainbox. Blotto sat in front of his sister, pathetically eager, panting with anticipation like a Labrador puppy.

But her opening words offered little comfort. 'We really are both feet in the quagmire this time, aren't we?'

'Surely though, Twinks, you know a way we can squirm out?'

The shake of her silken blonde hair dashed his hopes. 'You know when the mater's got her fangs into a notion, she hangs on like a crocodile with a fisherman's leg. If she's decided you're going to be grafted on to this Mary Chapstick, then you'd better get Tweedling ironing your morning dress straight away.'

The downcast expression that greeted this was more than she could bear. 'But don't don your worry-boots, Blotto. We'll find a way out as quick as a lizard's lick.'

'Oh, will we?' said Blotto, at once re-energized. There was a silence, then he asked, 'What is it?'

'Sorry, me old trombone? What's what?'

'The way out of it that you've found.'

'Ah.' The rosiness heightened on her delicate cheeks. 'I haven't exactly found it yet.'

'Oh.' The thermometer of Blotto's feelings once again sank to the bottom of the tube. He wasn't used to his sister being nonplussed. Normally he would present her with a problem and she'd be instantly plussed, coming up with an immediate solution.

21

'But I will!' Twinks announced triumphantly. 'And then everything will all be larksissimo again!'

'Hoopee-doopee,' cried Blotto, suitably cheered.

'I'll just give the problemette a little cogitette, and then we'll be once again rolling in camomile lawns. In fact . . .' she removed one hand from her cocoa mug and raised a jubilant finger '. . . I've already found the solution!'

'Toad-in-the-hole!' exclaimed Blotto. 'You've got a brain as big as the entire night sky. Twinks, you really are the nun's nightie. So what is the solution?'

'The mater only wants you to marry this Yankee-doodle-dandy because we have no other means of paying for the new plumbing and the restoration of the paintings . . .'

'On the same hymn-sheet as you on that, Twinks me old kipper.'

'. . . so all we have to do is to find another way of getting the necessary jingle-jangle and the threat of transatlantic matrimony will suddenly waft off the horizon.'

'Good ticket! I don't know how you manage to come up with stuff like that, Twinks. Why can't I do it?'

From the nursery onwards his sister had always been too kind to answer that question.

'So . . .' asked Blotto, 'what is the other way of getting the necessary jingle-jangle?'

'Ah,' said Twinks. 'That's the bit I haven't quite worked out yet.'

Blotto was . . . not on the scale that the Dowager Duchess might have been, nor as destructively, but still rather *disappointed* in his sister.

It was Blotto's view that life in England was pretty damn well organized. Though being Church of England his belief in a God was a little ill-defined, he really would have liked to congratulate the someone or something who'd sorted everything out so well. The cricket season started in April and ran through to September. The foxhunting season started in November and ran through to April. And for people like Blotto who saw no purpose in taking a break in the sporting calendar, there was always cubhunting available in October.

The flood at Tawcester Towers had happened at the beginning of April, a time of year that Blotto had always found particularly juicy. Foxhunting nearly over and with his splendid horse Mephistopheles looking forward to his summer hols, before Blotto stretched an endless vista of days at the wicket, as back-to-back games of cricket followed their snail tracks through the balmy laziness of summer.

But suddenly that blissful prospect was threatened. The appalling thought came to him that this might be his last summer of cricket, that he might be fated to spend the rest of his life in a country for whose denizens the pinnacle of sporting activity was rounders.

More awful even than that was the possibility that, given the urgency of the Tawcester Towers financial situation, the Dowager Duchess might decree that his marriage should take place before the end of the cricket season. Blotto had been taught from boyhood that it wasn't 'on' for boddos to blub, but that thought did bring to his eye an unrestrainable tear.

And just when he thought that there were no depths lower to which his spirits could plummet, the Dowager Duchess announced that Luther P. Chapstick III and his daughter Mary would be joining the party at Tawcester Towers the following weekend.

4

A Ticklish Problem with a Guest List

'There is a person on the telephone, Your Grace,' announced Grimshaw, the Tawcester Towers butler, 'who wishes you to come and speak to him.'

'To come and speak to him?' echoed the Dowager Duchess, doing a very passable impression of the Wrath of God.

There was only one telephone in Tawcester Towers. It was placed on a table in the high draughty hallway. The Dowager Duchess never answered it or was summoned to it. If one of her social equals rang for her, the message would be passed on and she would return the call to belittle the friend at a time of her choosing. If she initiated a call, that would also be when she wanted to do it. She would lift the receiver and bellow into it, terrifying the poor girl on the local exchange. (Her voice was of the kind that sounded as though it could talk to friends in the Colonies without the intervention of a telephone.)

But no one had ever before had the temerity to summon the Dowager Duchess out to take a call in the hall.

She turned on her butler a look that could set a tiger's teeth chattering at fifty paces. 'Have you taken in nothing, Grimshaw, in all the years you have been serving here at Tawcester Towers?'

'I can assure you, Your Grace, I have taken in a great deal.'

The look she now turned on him would not just have chattered the tiger's teeth, it would have killed the creature stone dead. 'Then why,' she bellowed, 'haven't you taken in the fact that I never go out into the hall to answer the telephone?'

'The gentleman at the other end of the line was very insistent, Your Grace.'

'No one is insistent to the Dowager Duchess of Tawcester!'

Her treatment of the butler had much in common with sandblasting, but Grimshaw stood up to the assault with remarkable courage (born of long practice). 'Well, I regret to inform you that this gentleman is, Your Grace.'

'And what is the name of this extraordinarily insolent gentleman?'

'Luther P. Chapstick III, Your Grace.'

'I'll come through to the hall straight away.'

*   *   *

'Duchess—hi!' The Dowager Duchess was too shocked by this greeting to say anything, so the meat-packing magnate continued from the other end of the line, 'Just to say that little Mary-Bobs and me are really looking forward to our weekend at Tawcester Towers.'

By now the Dowager Duchess was capable

25

of a civil reply. 'I can assure you the family is looking forward to it just as much as you are, Mr Chapstick.'

'Hey, where's all this formality come from? Call me Luther.'

Though anxious to please, the Dowager Duchess was not *that* anxious to please. 'I am not in the habit, Mr Chapstick, of using a first-name form of address to people I have not met.'

'We're meeting now, Duchess. On the old blower. So let's relax. You call me "Luther" and ... what should I call you?'

'"Your Grace" is normally regarded as adequate to the situation.'

'OK, have it your way, Duchess. Now, this weekend ... I wanted to check out the arrangements.'

'I can assure you, Mr Chapstick, that the arrangements will be entirely appropriate to the occasion. Some rooms in the house will be closed due to recent flood damage, but otherwise the customary high standards of Tawcester Towers hospitality will of course be maintained.'

'Yeah, but what's bugging me is ... who the other guests're going to be?'

'There will not be any other guests, Mr Chapstick. I thought ... given our hopes for a closer bond in the future ...' it was agony for her to utter such words '... this weekend should be a splendid opportunity for our two families to meet in an atmosphere of informal intimacy.' She said this, though never in her life had she aspired to either informality or intimacy.

'Hey, that's not the deal I'm after, Duchess,' said Luther P. Chapstick III.

'I beg your pardon?' The Dowager Duchess was affronted. People of her class did not make 'deals'.

'Listen, it's cards on the table time here. I know the reason why you want to marry your goofball of a son to my daughter . . .'

The Dowager Duchess had never heard the expression before, but its meaning was self-evident. And she couldn't help feeling that, when it came to her younger son, 'goofball' was probably an apposite description.

'You're after my money, and that's fair enough, because I got squillions of the old greenbacks. We're not kids, Duchess. We're in a process of negotiation here. Now I do a hell of a lotta negotiation in my business and I never like being bilked on a deal. You're selling me a steer or a heifer I want to know I'm getting my money's worth.'

'Mr Chapstick, my son Devereux is neither a steer nor a heifer.'

'I was just using that as an example, Duchess. Let's face the facts. The deal is: we get this marriage off the ground, you get money to maintain Tawcester Towers, Mary and I get a way into the British aristocracy.'

'Well, your daughter would certainly get a title, but there'd be nothing of that kind for you, Mr Chapstick.'

'You say that, you don't know it. Listen, Duchess, I'm divorced. I offloaded Mary's momma way back. She was becoming a bit of a liability. So I'm a free agent. I'm back in the meat market. And who's to say I shouldn't follow in my little Mary-Bobs' footsteps and marry a British aristocrat too?'

The Dowager Duchess could think of a lot of

27

people who could say he shouldn't. Everyone in civilized society.

'So I want to make connections, Duchess. I want to meet other aristocrats this weekend. So fix it—right?'

'Mr Chapstick, are you telling me whom I should invite for the weekend?' asked a flabbergasted Dowager Duchess. 'Are you dictating my own guest list to me?'

'Sure am. Come off it, you lot in the British aristocracy all know each other—most of you are related to each other. Pick up the blower, issue a few invites.'

'I am afraid, Mr Chapstick, it will not be possible for me to—'

'Make the calls, Duchess.' His voice took on the steely quality that was essential for anyone wishing to make it big in the Chicago meat-packing industry. 'You don't provide me with a nice house party of aristocrats this weekend, my Mary-Bobs goes off and marries someone else . . . taking all my mazuma with her. Gottit?'

'I've got it, Mr Chapstick,' said the Dowager Duchess.

*   *   *

'Well, Twinks?' she demanded.

The summons to attend the Dowager Duchess in the Blue Morning Room had been addressed to her daughter alone. Twinks immediately understood what that meant. This was not to be a dressing-down, not another occasion for her mother to express disappointment. This time there was a problem to be faced which required intellect.

28

Which is why there had been no summons for Blotto, in whose devastatingly handsome cranium the traditional percentages of brain and bone had been reversed.

'I agree we have a problemette,' said Twinks. 'But surely there are some minor aristocracy that you could invite? Poor relations, we've always got plenty of those.'

'The trouble with poor relations,' said the Dowager Duchess, 'is that they're constantly in touch with rich relations.'

'Yes, but only to ask them for money.'

'Not only that, Twinks. They ask for money, yes, but they also pass on gossip. If we invite any genuine aristocrats, the news that we've had the Chapsticks to stay at Tawcester Towers will be round everyone who matters within hours. We might as well publish the details in the Court Circular.'

'But the fact that Blotto's being lined up to twiddle the reef-knot with Mary Chapstick is going to come out some time. When the wedding invitations are issued, if not before ...' Twinks looked sharply at her mother as a rather ghastly thought came into her mind. 'That is, unless you were hoping to get him married off in America with nobody this side of the Atlantic knowing a blind bezonger about it ...?'

'That had been my intention, yes,' admitted the Dowager Duchess.

'But somebody's going to do up the buttons after the wedding. When Blotto comes back here to Tawcester Towers with his new bride.'

'Only if he does come back here to Tawcester Towers with his new bride.'

Twinks turned another sharp look on her mother, unwilling to believe the full enormity of what had just been said. She hadn't expected sentimentality, but banishing Blotto from his beloved home for ever ... well, that was a whole new level of stenchdom ... and not the kind of hand one expected to be dealt by an Aged P.

Still, this wasn't the moment to argue with the Dowager Duchess about that. Twinks would apply her considerable brainpower to the problemette later. First priority was the weekend's guest list.

'I think I may see a solutionette, Mater,' she said.

The Dowager Duchess sat back in her Chippendale throne, marginally relaxed. She knew that her brilliant daughter could see a way round most things.

'Your dilemma is,' Twinks continued slowly, 'that you are honour bound this weekend to provide Luther P. Chapstick III with a house party of the right sort of people ... but you don't want the fact that you are even entertaining him here at Tawcester Towers ever to be found out by the right sort of people.'

'That's what I just told you, Twinks,' said the Dowager Duchess testily.

'I'm sorry, Mater, I was piecing the situation together.'

'Well, could you piece it together a bit quicker?'

'Tickey-tockey.' There was a moment's silence, then a slow smile brought even more radiance to Twinks's perfect face as she announced, 'So what you need, Mater, is some of the wrong sort of people to impersonate the right sort of people.'

'To pretend to be members of the aristocracy?'

'Bong on the nose, Mater.'

'But no one would ever get away with it,' objected the Dowager Duchess. 'If there's one thing our sort of people are good at it's spotting the rotten fish in the barrel. Over the years lots of petty, jumped-up parvenus have tried to pass themselves off as the genuine article, but people of our sort always know when the Stilton's iffy.'

'I agree, Mater. People of our sort do. But the whole point is that we're not dealing with people of our sort.'

'Sorry? Not on the same page.' Sometimes Twinks's mother could be almost as slow of perception as her younger son.

'Luther P. Chapstick III,' she explained patiently, 'comes from the United States of America, a landmass which prides itself on having no aristocracy. I doubt if he could spot the kitten in a basket of puppies, let alone a genuine aristocrat from a leadpenny one.'

A sliver of sunshine crept across the Dowager Duchess's craggy features as she caught on to her daughter's drift. But it was quickly extinguished as she saw a new obstacle rearing its head. 'But where in the world are we going to find leadpenny aristocrats? I know Harrods claims to have "everything, for everyone, everywhere", but I don't believe even they stock 'em.'

'We don't have to look as far as Harrods, Mater. We have what we're looking for right here in Tawcester Towers.'

'Do we? Who? How?' The Dowager Duchess's words rang out like gunshots.

'You know Harvey?'

'Harvey the housemaid?'

'Yes, Mater. The one who has an "arrangement"

31

with Grimshaw.'

'I have no idea to what you are referring,' the Dowager Duchess lied. Everyone at Tawcester Towers knew that the butler and housemaid shared an 'arrangement' of an intimate nature not formalized by a sacrament of the church, but nobody above stairs would have lacked so much breeding as to mention it. Below stairs the 'arrangement' was referred to frequently, and in considerably more robust, not to say vulgar, terms.

'Well, I happen to know,' said Twinks, 'that before Harvey started skivvying here, she went by another name.'

'Really?'

'She was called "Rosie Caramella" . . .'

'Good heavens.'

'"The Cheeky Chanteuse". Harvey, Mater, used to be an actress.'

'*An actress!!!*' the Dowager Duchess echoed in appalled tones. She was about to ask why she had never been informed before of this appalling news, to expatiate on the awfulness of someone of such low moral standing sullying the corridors of Tawcester Towers, and to call Grimshaw to arrange for Harvey's immediate dismissal, when she suddenly realized the import of her daughter's words.

In a voice that was gently intrigued, she repeated, 'An actress, did you say, Twinks?'

5

Amateur Dramatics

'Oh, blimey, Your Grace, yes. I've played lots of toffs.'

Harvey's voice was as Cockney as a plate of jellied eels with pearl buttons. Though she stood respectfully enough in front of her employer in the Blue Morning Room, she was far from daunted by the Dowager Duchess. There was something challenging in the way she jutted her hip. And while the typical housemaid was often not much more than a girl, Harvey was considerably older. (Her staying in that junior role in the Tawcester Towers below stairs hierarchy was something engineered by Grimshaw.) Her uniform too, though in the traditional black relieved by the white of her cap and apron, looked different. The skirt was very much shorter than those worn by the other housemaids and it revealed a considerable expanse of tight black stocking (something else engineered by Grimshaw).

About Harvey there hung an indefinable, almost subversive quality. The Dowager Duchess could not have recognized that quality—let alone put a name to it—if it had leapt up and bitten her on the knee. Twinks, a modern girl not afraid to call a spade a garden implement, would have been equally unafraid to call the quality by its proper name: 'IT'. Or, even more daringly . . . sex appeal.

Though the ancient aristocrat did not possess a lorgnette, when the Dowager Duchess peered

33

at people it was as if through one. And it was that lorgnettish peer which she now focused on the over-ripe housemaid. 'Forgive my mentioning it, Harvey, but people of my breeding tend to speak in a rather different manner than that which you employ.'

'Oh yeah, but that's where the acting comes in, innit, Your Grace? Before I went on the halls, I done lots of theatre. And a good few of the plays I was in was about toffs . . . lords, ladies, you know. Public couldn't get enough of them.'

'I wonder why that is, Harvey.'

'Well, I think for one thing, Your Grace, everyone has always been fascinated by the doings of their betters . . .'

'I suppose that is reasonable, yes,' the Dowager Duchess conceded.

'. . . and then again, everyone likes a good laugh, don't they?'

The Dowager Duchess bridled. 'Are you suggesting that members of the theatre-going public find the activities of people of my breeding amusing?'

Harvey was about to give a reply in the affirmative, but catching a firm headshake from Twinks, transmuted it into a negative. 'Oh no, Your Grace. I'm sure they all know their place.'

'Good,' rumbled the Dowager Duchess. 'Maybe, Harvey, given that you say you have spent much of your time impersonating your betters, you could vouchsafe me a sample of what you imagine to be the speech of the upper classes.'

'Of course, Your Grace,' said the housemaid in her customary Cockney, which vanished as she continued, 'I think it's absolutely shocking the kind

34

of jumped-up lowlife to whom this government is peddling peerages these days.'

Twinks could not believe her ears. The voice that Harvey had produced was not just similar to that of the Dowager Duchess; it was an exact copy. And, what's more, the sentiments expressed were ones which she had heard verbatim from her mother's mouth on more than one occasion. Twinks reckoned that Harvey's impersonation of her employer must be a very popular variety turn below stairs.

But any resemblance was lost on the Dowager Duchess. 'Hmm . . . I don't believe I've ever heard anyone of my breeding speak like that.'

'Hmm . . . I don't believe I've ever heard anyone of my breeding speak like that,' echoed Harvey perfectly, but rather cheekily to Twinks's mind.

'No, no, completely wrong,' said the Dowager Duchess. 'Nobody talks like that. Anyway, Harvey, what you were using there is an old person's voice. Could you attempt the upper-class locution of someone nearer your own age?'

'I most certainly could.'

Twinks was again shocked, but this time by the cut-glass perfection of the housemaid's vowels. The shock redoubled when she realized that the new voice sounded exactly like her own. Maybe the Dowager Duchess wasn't the only character featuring in Harvey's below stairs music hall routine.

There was a long silence while the old woman cogitated, then she pronounced, 'Excellent. That voice would certainly pass in the best of circles. You may regard yourself employed, Harvey.'

'That's all very well, but what's the money, Your

Grace?' For such practical matters the housemaid had dropped back into her customary Cockney.

'Money?' echoed the appalled Dowager Duchess. 'But you are already in receipt of your wages, Harvey.'

'That's as may be, Your Grace, but I gets my wages for being a housemaid, not being a theatrical. Being a theatrical's over and above, and if I'm doing over and above I want to get paid for it. That's what I always tells Grimshaw when he wants over and above.'

Whether this last sentence referred to Harvey's duties as a housemaid or something else was not a question the Dowager Duchess would ever have thought to ask. Instead, she went on, 'Anyway, I am not prepared to discuss remuneration until you can guarantee me more than just your own services.'

'How d'you mean, Your Grace?'

'I mean, I do not need just one impersonator of the aristocracy. I require six. Do you have amongst your acquaintance other people of equivalent skills to your own?'

'Course I do. Give me half an hour on the blower and I'll have five more of my mates from the halls here by lunchtime tomorrow. Wodjer want—two more ladies and three gents?'

'That, I believe, would meet my requirements. And they are all of the same competence as yourself?'

'If you didn't know, you'd never tell 'em apart from the real thing. You'd think every one of them'd been born with a golden spoon in his mush.'

'Very well, Harvey. Rather than request elucidation of the meaning of the word "mush", I will rely on you to get on with making the necessary

36

arrangements.' There followed a seismic clearing of the aristocratic throat. 'And now perhaps we should discuss the sordid business of reimbursement.'

The negotiations were ferocious and protracted. Harvey had honed her skills on skinflint theatre managers, but the Dowager Duchess too showed—for someone in whose presence money was never mentioned—a surprising aptitude for horse-trading.

Eventually an agreement was reached. 'It is a considerably larger sum than I was anticipating paying,' said the Dowager Duchess. This was not difficult; she had anticipated paying nothing. And indeed, if she'd had any more money to pay Harvey and her troupe of travelling players, the necessity for the subterfuge would not have arisen. 'But I am prepared to part with such a large sum only on one condition.'

'And what's that, Your Grace?' asked Harvey suspiciously. She was very pleased with the deal that had just been negotiated, and didn't want to see it in any way diluted.

'The condition, Harvey, is that neither you nor any of your associates ever dares to mention this transaction to another living soul.'

Harvey's suspicion lifted. 'Don't you worry about that, Your Grace. We'll all be schtum and mum. We'll keep as quiet about it as a butler slipping into bed.' And if Harvey didn't know about that simile, then nobody did.

*   *   *

'All of these clothes are wrong,' announced the Dowager Duchess as she inspected the costume parade of counterfeit aristocrats the following

37

evening.

Harvey, dressed in an off-the-shoulder knee-length evening gown with beaded overdress, swung her strings of pearls angrily as she took issue with her employer. 'I can assure you they are absolutely kosher, Your Grace. They was bought from the best costumiers in London, what pride themselves on getting every detail right. What we're wearing's toff's schmutter, no two ways about that.'

'It is not the garments themselves that are wrong. It is the fact that they all look brand new. No self-respecting personage of my breeding would be seen dead in something that looks new. And those gentlemen in their tweed suits and evening wear ... I see no sign of elbow patches, frayed cuffs or silk reveres turning a little green with age. No, a genuine aristocrat would spot this assemblage as leadpenny straight away.'

'We are not dealing with genuine aristocrats, though,' her daughter pointed out. 'Only Americans.'

'That's not the point, Twinks,' riposted the Dowager Duchess. '*I* wouldn't feel at ease surrounded by people in brand new clothes.'

Twinks did not pursue the argument further, but made the sensible suggestion that their new guests could be adequately costumed from the wardrobes of herself, her mother, her two brothers and the late Duke. The changes were duly made, and the procession of iffy aristocrats was reassembled. They looked distinctly scruffier and therefore much more like the real thing. This time they passed the Dowager Duchess's scrutiny.

Next she auditioned their voices and, though always ready to criticize, she found there was little she could fault. What one or two of the actors said was rather too polite for genuine members of the upper classes, but she put them right on that and soon all of them were speaking with authentic aristocratic rudeness. 'Also talk loudly,' she advised. 'It would never occur to someone of my breeding that there was anyone else in the room.'

Only an hour or so later the Dowager Duchess pronounced herself satisfied. Names and identities had been established, with a lot of help from Twinks, who had provided each of the counterfeit peers with convincing histories. As a result, amidst the dukes, earls and minor baronets, the room now contained two dowager duchesses. The genuine one was seated beside a leadpenny one, the Dowager Duchess of Framlington, formerly known as Harvey. (The story that Twinks had provided for her was that her husband the Duke of Framlington had lost his life in the latest big dust-up with the Boche, having made the uncharacteristic mistake of being close to his men when they went over the top.)

'I think we've done rather well, don't you?' pronounced the chatelaine of Tawcester Towers to her disguised housemaid.

'Of why you should imagine that I have any interest in what you think I have no perception,' replied the Dowager Duchess of Framlington frostily.

'Very good, very good,' said the Dowager Duchess of Tawcester.

And something very like a beam slowly crackled across her craggy features.

*   *   *

Twinks couldn't find her brother in the house, but she had a pretty good idea where he might be. At times of stress, Blotto's two immediate resources were cricket and hunting. Well, there wasn't any cricket planned till the weekend, and the hunting season was almost over. But if he couldn't actually hunt, he could still commune with his hunter Mephistopheles. Blotto was probably closer to the horse than to anything else in his life, other than his cricket bat. Certainly closer to Mephistopheles than he was to any human being, with the possible exception of Twinks.

She heard her brother's voice as she approached the stable block and lingered a moment before revealing herself, to hear what Blotto was saying. His voice was uncharacteristically doomy.

'It really is the flea's armpit, Mephistopheles,' he was complaining. 'The mater's once again got me entered for the Matrimonial Stakes and there's no way I'm going to save my chitterlings this time. I'm in the deepest gluepot ever—right up to the neck, glue lapping round the old chin, don't you know.'

Mephistopheles let out a whinny of deep sympathy.

'And what's really put lumps in my custard is that the filly the mater's lined up for me is a spoffing American! Which means I'm going to be packed off to America like some remittance man and never allowed to pongle my way back to Blighty. I'll probably have to leave you here, Mephistopheles.' His voice broke as the enormity hit him. 'Couldn't risk taking a fine specimen like you over the Pond. Yankees don't do any proper hunting, not as we'd recognize it. And their national game is spoffing

40

rounders! If they got their hands on you, they'd probably get you cavorting around in some Wild West show as quick as a lizard's lick, with some Indian chief doing trick shooting off your back. Oh, it's all so murdey. I don't think I've ever felt this vinegared off in my entire puff.'

Mephistopheles snorted further sympathy and, rather than listen to more of her brother's mournful litany, Twinks entered the stable.

'Listen, Blotto, me old brass bedstead, pull off your worry-boots. I've got an idea that'll really bisect the bull's eye!'

'To get me out of this matrimonial treacle tin?'

'Hope so. Certainly worth having a bong at it. Listen, you know the mater and I have been drilling Harvey and her theatricals on their country house etiquette . . .'

'Yes.'

'Well, I've been providing the poor droplets with personal histories . . .'

'Sorry, not on the same page . . .'

'I've been setting them up with backgrounds, when their peerages started, where their country seats are, where they went to school and all that rombooley . . .'

'Ah. I read your semaphore.'

'Well, Blotto, I have invented a duke for you.'

'I beg your pardon?'

'One of these actor johnnies is not bad looking. Not as tasty a slice of redcurrant cheesecake as you are, obviously, but then who is?' Her brother blushed. He was always terribly embarrassed if anyone mentioned his looks. 'Anyway, his name's Briscoe Daubeney-Vere—or at least that's what he calls himself. A lot of these actor johnnies change

41

their names. But what I've done with Briscoe Daubeney-Vere's personal history is: I've bumped him up the peerage a bit. He's now the Duke of Godalming, so everything should be jollissimo, shouldn't it?'

'Sorry, Twinks, you've lost me again.'

'Listen, Luther P. Chapstick III is coming to Tawcester Towers this weekend because he wants a cheap steerage ticket into the British aristocracy. His daughter Mary's being lined up to breed with you . . .'

'Which is a total candle-snuffer,' said Blotto, reminded of his ghastly fate.

'But suppose, when the fair Americanette comes here, she meets the handsome young Duke of Godalming? You're just the younger son of a duke, Blotters, not the whole clangdumble. She marries you, she doesn't get to become a duchess, does she? Don't you think there's at least an each-way punt that Mary Chapstick—and her father—are going to be more interested in the Duke of Godalming than they are in you?'

'But surely this Daubeney-Vere pineapple isn't a real duke?'

'He knows that. You know that. The mater knows that. I know that. But the Chapsticks don't know it, do they?'

As Blotto took a firm hold on the lifeline his sister had thrown him, a beam irradiated his handsome features and he cried, 'By Denzil, Twinks, you know you really are the lark's larynx!'

6

An Impromptu Dance

Though Blotto never expected to find in a woman the purity of line he saw in Mephistopheles or in his cricket bat, he couldn't deny that Mary Chapstick was astonishingly pretty. She was built on more generous lines than his sister, and her bobbed hair was nearly black. She was dressed in the height of fashion—London's couturiers must have been under siege in the days before her visit to Tawcester Towers—and the current style showed her bare arms and stockinged legs to advantage. The extensive strings of pearls looped around her neck suggested that she came from one of those families where money was not a problem (though breeding clearly was).

That such a creature could be the daughter of Luther P. Chapstick III suggested, by the law of averages, that his long-divorced wife must have been a being of extraordinary beauty. Where the daughter was sylphlike, the father was gross. Where her features were small and refined, his looked as though his face had been put too near a fire and melted. Whereas Mary Chapstick brought to mind images of a gazelle, her father's nearest equivalent in the animal kingdom would have been a warthog.

But, as became clear at dinner on the Friday, the first evening of their stay, Luther P. Chapstick III's table manners did not aspire to warthog standards. It was as if the delivery of each course acted as a starting pistol for a new race, and nothing must be

43

allowed to stand in the way of his finishing before the other guests had even started. And if such haste led inevitably to splattering of food and drink over his chin and evening wear . . . well, that was just the price that had to be paid.

Had he been at a table surrounded by genuine aristocrats, this might have been noticed less. There are plenty of peers of the realm over a certain age for whom untidy eating is a way of life. Indeed, in some circles—notably the House of Lords— to add to the general fraying and aging of their garments, souvenirs of dinners past on lapels and waistcoats are considered de rigueur. But though their borrowed clothes might have sported such gastronomic badges of honour, the decorous way in which the counterfeit aristocrats gathered round the Tawcester Towers dining table that first evening addressed their food only served to show up the messiness of Luther P. Chapstick III's eating.

His breathing, too, echoed that of a warthog. Perhaps some malformation of his throat— or maybe just a lifetime of barking orders to underlings—had left the meat-packing magnate with a propensity to growl and grunt and snort with every breath that he took.

Twinks had had some input into the Dowager Duchess's seating plan and on the placement cards Luther P. Chapstick III had been seated next to the Dowager Duchess of Framlington. Harvey gloried in her new role and was unashamedly overt in her eyelash-fluttering come-ons to the guest at her side. Luther P. Chapstick III clearly had no objection to being treated in this way. In fact, his enjoyment of Harvey's behaviour was as strong as Grimshaw's aggravation at it. The butler could not step out of his subservient role to reprimand the provocative housemaid, but those who knew him very well—like Harvey herself—could detect in the smallest flicker of an eyebrow the intensity of his fury. That did not, however, deter the Dowager Duchess of Framlington. Indeed, it seemed to spur her on to a greater openness of flirtation.

Twinks's placement had placed Mary Chapstick between the Duke of Godalming (known to his intimates until the previous day as Briscoe Daubeney-Vere) and her brother. Blotto had pleaded to be put as far away from his proposed bride as possible but, though Twinks had some sway with her mother, the Dowager Duchess was never likely to have accepted that suggestion. But at least her positioning enabled Mary Chapstick to compare the witty volubility of the Duke of Godalming with the tongue-tied incoherence of Devereux Lyminster. Blotto saw the point of his sister's plan and played the tongue-tied incoherence card for all he was worth.

'Er . . . dinner,' he'd said when the ladies were all seated and his own chair had been pushed in.

'Yes, dinner,' Mary Chapstick had agreed.

'Um . . . Er . . . Best meal of the day . . .'

'Yes.'

'Erm . . . Uh . . . Though lunch isn't bad . . .'

'True.'

'Mm . . . Well . . . Hmm . . . Though there's a lot to be said for a good breakfast.'

'Oh, you're so right.'

'Mmm . . . Do you like cricket?'

'What, you mean the cute little insect that hops about on the hearth?'

'Hmmm . . .'

Having shot his conversational bolt, Blotto was content to spend the rest of the meal in silence, avoiding stern looks from his mother encouraging him to make more effort. Meanwhile, Mary Chapstick listened to the daring deeds of the charming Duke of Godalming (all remembered from aristocratic parts he had played on a variety of stages). She seemed, to Blotto's mind, to be falling under the spell of the young duke in an extremely satisfying way.

And Luther P. Chapstick III was falling further under the spell of the seductive Dowager Duchess of Framlington. And Grimshaw was seething inwardly.

Twinks was struck by the fact that the standard of conversation that evening was rather better than that normally experienced at Tawcester Towers dinner parties. The counterfeit aristocrats, all quoting from plays they had been in, provided much wittier dialogue than she had ever heard their genuine counterparts come up with.

She particularly enjoyed one exchange between the two dowager duchesses. Her mother was pontificating about 'the Tawcester family tradition', when she was interrupted by the Dowager Duchess of Framlington, who said, 'Of course, when you speak of "family tradition", you refer to a fairly recent family tradition.'

'I beg your pardon?' demanded the Dowager Duchess of Tawcester, to whom interruption was a novel experience.

'Well, the Tawcester peerage only dates from the twelfth century, doesn't it?' The question was asked with a supercilious smile. 'Whereas my family, the Framlingtons, came over with the Conqueror.'

The baleful look that the Dowager Duchess of Tawcester focused on her upstart housemaid showed that Grimshaw wasn't the only one Harvey's behaviour was causing to seethe inwardly.

*   *   *

It was Twinks's suggestion before the ladies withdrew that, after the gentlemen had enjoyed their port, brandy and cigars, the younger members of the house party should reassemble in the Pink Drawing Room for informal dancing to music from the gramophone. Part of the aim was to demonstrate to the Chapsticks how jolly life at a Tawcester Towers house party could be, but that was not her only motive. In her conversations with Briscoe Daubeney-Vere about the background they were inventing for him, the actor had revealed that much of his work had been as a song-and-dance-man in operettas and revues.

Twinks saw this as a clincher. She loved her brother dearly, and was proud of his many skills, but she knew that dancing was not among them. The moment music started to play, Blotto instantly developed more left feet than the customary allocation. Though a dancing instructor had come to Tawcester Towers to train them from an early age, while Twinks was soon as accomplished on the dance floor as she was in every other arena, her brother had made as little progress as a cockroach in custard.

So, thought Twinks, Blotto having proved an empty revolver on the conversational front, all that was needed was for Mary Chapstick to witness the comparative dancing skills of the two young

47

men for her to have no choice but to fall into the arms of the dashing, witty and light-footed Duke of Godalming. Then her brother would be saved from a lifetime's exile in the forbidding vastness of America.

Twinks's plan looked as if it was going to work. Once male and female guests were together again in the Pink Drawing Room, the Dowager Duchess had played into her daughter's hands by insisting that Blotto should have the first dance with Mary Chapstick. Vindictively, but for her brother's own good, Twinks adjusted the gramophone's horn, wound the mechanism up, and slipped from its paper sleeve a record of the Charleston. Though Blotto might almost have passed muster dancing a waltz, the Charleston was guaranteed to make him move like a giraffe with a wooden leg.

And so it proved. While he could handle a cricket bat or Mephistopheles with perfect balance and precision, on the dance floor all Blotto's coordination deserted him. Had the other guests present been real aristocrats, they would have laughed at his assault on the Charleston. He was only saved from total ridicule by the fact that they were actors playing parts, who, mistakenly, believed that members of the British upper classes were nice to each other.

Blotto's humiliation was complete when Mary Chapstick, having politely but firmly refused the offer of a second dance, was swept up into the arms of the Duke of Godalming for an expert and energetic Black Bottom.

With a look at her son which expressed deep disappointment, the Dowager Duchess announced to anyone prepared to listen that she was going to bed.

'A good idea,' commented the Dowager Duchess of Framlington. 'You of all people need your beauty sleep.'

The real Dowager Duchess focused on the false one a stare that could have flambéed a banana. Harvey ignored it, as she ignored the comparably combustible look from Grimshaw, and accepted Luther P. Chapstick III's invitation to dance. Soon the couple were involved in an energetically intimate foxtrot.

Blotto deposited himself in a seat next to his sister. (She had eschewed dancing because, though all the young men had instantly fallen in love with her, she didn't want to cause any trouble by showing favours to her inferiors.)

'This is beezer, Twinks me old biscuit barrel! Spoffing brilliant idea of yours! Give that pony a rosette! Mary Chapstick's fallen for the Duke of Godalming hook, line and stinker.'

'Sinker.'

'What?'

'Never mind. No, Blotto me old gumdrop, all the ducks are lining up. There seems to be an attraction there.'

'Attraction? They're all over each other like the measles.' Blotto looked at the dancers for an illustration of his words, but saw no sign of the couple. 'Toad-in-the-hole, though. Where've they gone?'

'They slipped out on to the terrace for some air.'

Blotto grinned hugely. It was all going better than he dared hope. For two young people to slip out on to a terrace to get some air . . . well, that was tantamount to being engaged, wasn't it? He felt the America-sized cloud above his head begin to dissipate.

'You really are the panda's panties, Twinks me old fondant fancy!'

'It's nothing,' his sister responded casually. 'It's just . . .' She stopped, her eye caught by some movement near the French windows. 'Oh, Mary Chapstick's just come back in.'

'Probably doesn't want to set tongues wagging too soon . . . let all the poor greengages wait till the official announcement in the Court Circular.'

'Yes, I wonder . . .' Twinks said as she picked up her silver beaded reticule. She sounded troubled. Blotto wondered what information her hypersensitive antennae had picked up this time. 'I'll just go out and see. You look after the gramophone for the moment, will you, Blotto?'

'Tickey-tockey.' He liked operating the machine—winding it up, putting a record on, placing the needle on its outermost groove. Amazing piece of equipment, he thought. A whole spoffing orchestra in a box. Right there in a boddo's sitting room. All you had to do was wind the thing up. Nobody would ever come up with an invention for reproducing music that was as clever as the gramophone.

*　　　*　　　*

Twinks felt a chill as she walked out on to the terrace, and it wasn't just the cool of the April evening. She looked to her left and saw a figure slumped over the balustrade.

It was the Duke of Godalming—or rather Briscoe Daubeney-Vere masquerading as the Duke of Godalming.

50

And though some blood still flowed from the wound in his throat, he was undoubtedly dead.

7

The Scene of the Crime

Twinks acted quickly and instinctively. She always carried a Scene of Crime kit in her reticule, and she took out its small torch to look at the dead man more closely.

There was a lot of blood from the wound, but it didn't look as though Briscoe Daubeney-Vere's throat had been cut. A cursory examination suggested to Twinks that he had been shot from a distance, the bullet severing his jugular vein and possibly, given the angle at which he had fallen, one of his carotid arteries too.

She made a quick estimate of the direction from which such a shot could have been fired and reckoned it might well have come from a small copse that lay beyond the ha-ha, some couple of hundred yards from the Tawcester Towers main building. She looked out to where she knew the copse to be, but could see nothing in the encroaching darkness.

She turned the thin beam of her torch to the shutter in front of which Briscoe Daubeney-Vere must have been standing, and was immediately rewarded by a splatter of blood surrounding something set deeply into the wood.

Extracting a small penknife from her reticule, Twinks held the torch in place with one hand while with the other she dug into the shutter.

In a matter of moments she had loosened and pulled out what she'd expected to find there. A bullet.

She focused the torch on her prize, and immediately recognized that it had been fired from an Accrington-Murphy PL23 hunting rifle.

Twinks slipped the bullet into an evidence bag, placed that in her reticule and went back into the Pink Drawing Room to arrange for the disposal of the body.

*　　*　　*

There was a routine to these things, and Twinks knew it well. Waking her mother was not part of that routine. The Dowager Duchess cherished her sleep (what Harvey had referred to impudently as her 'beauty sleep') and would have been extremely annoyed to have it interrupted by trivialities. The death of a houseguest—particularly one who wasn't even a genuine aristocrat—would definitely have come into that category.

Tawcester Towers had a long history of the discreet disposal of bodies. In the early days of the family history a good few mutilated serfs had found their way into unmarked graves on the extensive estate. The wicked Duke 'Black Rupert' had been an enthusiastic despoiler of virgins and the bodies of many of those had conveniently disappeared. The same fate had awaited a young housemaid crushed in the Tawcester Towers library by a falling bust of Homer in the 1820s.

The basic rule was: if the dead person was from below stairs or otherwise insignificant, their body should be disposed of without troubling the proper authorities. Chief Inspector Trumbull and Sergeant Knatchbull of the Tawcestershire Constabulary were far too busy with such urgent cases as cats stuck up trees or the theft of radishes from a church's harvest festival to be sidetracked by a case of murder at Tawcester Towers. Besides, bringing such a complex case to their attention could not fail to aggravate their perpetual condition of bafflement. It was only human charity to keep them in the dark about such matters.

So, having concluded her examination of the crime scene, Twinks slipped back into the Pink Drawing Room to have a discreet word with Grimshaw. The butler detailed the appropriate staff to tidy up the terrace, and within an hour the mortal remains of Briscoe Daubeney-Vere were buried deep in a freshly dug bed of thyme in the Tawcester Towers herb garden.

Having given Grimshaw his instructions, Twinks reckoned that the only person likely to be concerned about the Duke of Godalming's disappearance was Mary Chapstick. She crossed the room to Blotto, still content with his role as record changer for the gramophone. 'If by any chance,' she whispered, 'Mary should ask you where the Duke of Godalming has gone, could you say that he's been called away urgently by the news of a fire at his country estate?'

'Tickey-tockey,' said Blotto. 'Tough Gorgonzola for the poor old pineapple, though, isn't it, having the family place burn down?'

'Blotters,' said his sister patiently, 'the Duke of Godalming does not possess a family place. He doesn't exist.' As she spoke them she realized just how completely accurate her words were. 'The man who's been coffinated is a music hall artiste called Briscoe Daubeney-Vere.'

'"Coffinated"?' Blotto repeated. 'Are you telling me the poor old greengage . . .'

But he was stopped by his sister putting a finger to her lips as Mary Chapstick approached. Moving discreetly away, Twinks heard the American girl ask the whereabouts of the Duke of Godalming. He gave the reply that his sister had recommended to him. Mary Chapstick, only for a moment disappointed by the news, immediately focused her attention on Blotto. Within seconds she had dragged him away from the security of his seat by the gramophone to introduce him to a new dance called the Flea Hop (for which he showed the same aptitude as the old dances).

Catching the look of anguish that her brother cast in her direction, Twinks realized the full implication of Briscoe Daubeney-Vere's death. There was no longer anything to distract Mary Chapstick from her single-minded pursuit of Blotto.

Her detective instincts alerted, she asked herself who could benefit from such a turn of events. For a moment she even wondered whether her mother had organized the murder. The Dowager Duchess was not given to sentimentality and, if it offered to bring about the salvation of Tawcester Towers, would have had no qualms about following such a course.

*   *   *

Blotto accompanied his sister the following morning after breakfast. She said they were just going to get

54

some air, but he knew from her manner that the walk had a more serious purpose.

Mary Chapstick had so monopolized Blotto for the remainder of the previous evening that brother and sister had had no opportunity for any tête-à-tête conversation, so as they walked across the neat lawns to the side of Tawcester Towers, Twinks brought him up to date on the fate of Briscoe Daubeney-Vere.

'Poor old greengage,' said Blotto in an appropriately condolent voice. 'I know masquerading as one of us when you're not the genuine article is a bit beyond the barbed wire, but I wouldn't have thought it was a reason to coffinate the poor thimble.'

'I don't think that was why he was shot,' said Twinks thoughtfully.

'But you do know the real reason . . . ?' Blotto prompted.

To his surprise Twinks said she didn't. He was so used to her zapping to solutions of crimes like a hare on roller skates that he couldn't help feeling a bit let down.

She was, however, striding very purposefully along a route different from their customary walks, so he asked her why.

'I checked the trajectory of the bullet that did for Daubeney-Vere, and I reckon we should be looking for the copse.'

'What, you mean Chief Inspector Trumbull and Sergeant Knatchbull?'

'No, not that kind of "cops", Blotto. "Copse" as in a small wood.'

'Ah, read your semaphore, Twinks me old collar stud. This copse over here, you mean?'

55

'The very same.'

Twinks paused at the beginning of the trees and squinted back at Tawcester Towers. Taking an eye-line on the terrace outside the Pink Drawing Room, she slid gracefully along the edge of the copse and then suddenly moved in.

'This is where the stencher shot from,' she announced, pointing to an area of trampled grass behind a tree. She moved towards it and, taking a magnifying glass from her reticule, examined the lower branches. 'Yes, see, the bark's a little abraded here. I think he rested the barrel of his rifle in this vee to steady his aim. With a target nearly a hundred yards away he'd have needed that. Given the fact that there are other branches he could have rested the gun on . . .' Twinks screwed up her azure eyes as she made the calculation '. . . our murderer's about five foot seven in height.'

She dropped down to examine the crushed grass behind the tree. 'But the indentations made by his feet suggest he carries a lot of weight, far more than the average boddo of five foot seven. He's positively corpulent, I'd say. And the lump of toadspawn was wearing a size 6 climbing boot with a ribbed sole.' She scrutinized the footprints more closely. 'The boot's not of British manufacture.'

'How for the love of strawberries do you know that?' asked her astonished brother.

'I am familiar with the sole patterns of all British bootmakers,' Twinks replied casually. 'I did in fact write a monograph on the subject.'

'Toad-in-the-hole!' said Blotto.

'No, our murderer was either wearing a boot of German manufacture . . . that distinctive W-shaped ribbing is used by the Plotzlein Jagengeschäft

56

in Regensburg ... ah, but of course they always feature the "PJ" monogram on their soles, don't they?'

'Do they?' murmured Blotto.

'So this boot must have been made by The Acme Shoe Company of Detroit, established by Engelbrecht Plotzlein after he emigrated from Regensburg in 1893 ... which taken together with *this* ...' She snatched something from the ground and held it up for her brother's inspection. 'Do you know what it is?'

'Looks like a cigarette end.'

'You're bong on the nose there, Blotto! But it's not just any old cigarette end. This is a K&J Gold Nugget cigarette, which, as you know ...' Blotto nodded feebly '... is an American brand.

'All of which makes me think,' Twinks concluded magnificently, 'that our murderer is a citizen of the United States ... which raises another possibility, doesn't it, Blotto?'

'Just tell me,' he pleaded, acknowledging his total incompetence at guessing games.

'It raises the possibility that our murderer might have made a mistake.'

'Does it?'

'Shooting from this distance after dark, he couldn't be very accurate. I think there's a strong chance that he killed Briscoe Daubeney-Vere by mistake. And his intended target was Mary Chapstick!'

Blotto received this news with profound gloom. He'd already got the American heiress stuck on to him like an unwanted corn plaster. But if her life was in danger at Tawcester Towers, then to uphold the family honour he would have to protect her.

And he knew from bitter experience how readily girls misinterpreted masculine protectiveness as a demonstration of love.

All his hopes of escaping the current gluepot had, he realized, died with Briscoe Daubeney-Vere. Farewell, hunting. Farewell, cricket. Farewell, Tawcester Towers. Now he was inevitably destined to spend the miserable remainder of his days in America.

Oh, broken biscuits, thought Blotto savagely.

8

An Unfair Dismissal

The absence of the Duke of Godalming was unremarked on throughout the Saturday. Those who needed an explanation were satisfied with the story about his estate being on fire, while Briscoe Daubeney-Vere's fellow thespians were having far too much fun playing their roles, and enjoying the fine food and wines that came with those roles, to give him a second thought.

As Blotto had feared, Mary Chapstick stuck on to him for the rest of the day like a leech, albeit a very pretty leech. She was clearly totally besotted. This was a common phenomenon that his sister had frequently had to explain to him. Though Blotto thought of himself as just a normal old greengage like any other, his combination of devastating looks, sporting prowess, breeding and perfect manners cut a swathe through the ranks of young women, rather as the recent difference of opinion with the nation's

Teutonic cousins had through the ranks of young men.

So, though on the Tawcester side marriage to Mary Chapstick would be seen only as a commercial necessity, for her it would clearly be a love match. She hung on Blotto's every word, which, given how tongue-tied he tended to become in the presence of the fair sex, didn't give her a lot to hang on.

Blotto himself kept devising excuses that would mean he had to part with Mary for a few hours' respite, only to remember that because there was quite possibly a man with a gun on the estate, he should stay at her side to guard her. It was for Blotto a long day of discomfort and frustration.

Inevitably the Dowager Duchess's placement once again had him seated beside the American girl at Saturday night's dinner. On that occasion he did manage to bridge the conversational gulf between them by explaining to her the laws of cricket. Again she hung on to every word, glad at last to have a few more to hang on to. Whether she understood any of them is another matter, but the tender tête-à-tête of the young couple was observed with great satisfaction by the Dowager Duchess and by Luther P. Chapstick III.

The behaviour of the other dinner guests was moving towards the raucous. As actors relax, they tend to become more at ease in their roles, and of course there is no more popular relaxant for actors than alcohol. The fine wines of the Tawcester Towers cellars encouraged a greater flamboyance in the performances of Harvey's troupe. Speaking loudly soon turned into shouting; mock arguments swelled into real arguments; bread rolls and, later, soft fruits were thrown about the dining room with wild abandon.

The Dowager Duchess watched all this with an expression that was as near as her face could do to benign. She congratulated herself on the skill of the actors she had employed—because of course she'd seen far worse behaviour from genuine aristocrats.

The counterfeit aristocrat enjoying her role more than any of the others was the Dowager Duchess of Framlington. Once again the placement had seated her next to Luther P. Chapstick III, and the growing intimacy of their exchanges could be measured by the frequency of the almost imperceptible tic of the brow above Grimshaw's watchful eyes.

For Blotto the day finally dragged to its weary close. He faced the Sunday with a little more optimism. His exegesis of the laws of cricket to Mary Chapstick had not been a random act. There was actually to be a match the following day. A hastily arranged fixture for the benefit of their American guests, a Tawcester Towers Gentlemen and Artisans eleven would take on a nomadic team composed mostly of writers and poets who gloried in the name of the Semi-Colons. Blotto could have got together an opposing team of classier credentials, Old Etonians and what-have-you, but the Dowager Duchess still insisted the Chapsticks had to be kept apart from real aristocrats. And she felt quite safe with the Semi-Colons. There was no danger any of them might have contacts in the real aristocracy. On her scale of values writers and poets were the scum of the earth, ranking around the same level as solicitors and bank managers.

At least Blotto's duties at the crease and in the field on the morrow would prevent him from having to spend every minute at the side of Mary Chapstick. But even that relieving prospect was overshadowed by a darker question. How many more carefree days of cricket would there be in his life? Was that fine all-rounder the Honourable Devereux Lyminster doomed to spend the rest of his days in the United States of America watching rounders?

*   *   *

Even in times of stress Blotto slept like an unusually comatose baby, but that night his slumbers were interrupted by the sound of a bedroom door closing along the landing. This was followed by the tramp of heavy footsteps and a growling, grunting noise that sounded not dissimilar to the breathing of Luther P. Chapstick III. But, Blotto reflected before slipping straight back to sleep, their American guest would have no cause to go that way along the landing. If he required the plumbing facilities they were in the other direction. The only destination beyond Blotto's own doorway was the last bedroom on the landing, which had been allocated to the Dowager Duchess of Framlington. And there was no reason why Luther P. Chapstick III would want to go in there.

Nor did Blotto notice at breakfast the next morning that the tic in the eyebrow of Grimshaw the butler was now moving with the frequency of a hummingbird's wings.

His preoccupation then was to entrust Twinks with the task of guarding Mary Chapstick from attempted assassination before abandoning himself to the pleasures of a day's cricket.

61

Of course it wasn't a proper game. One of the things Mary Chapstick had found hardest to understand from Blotto's explanation of the previous evening was that ideally the process took five days. The idea of a contest restricted to, say, three hours for each side's innings—which was how the Sunday's match would be organized—was obviously a pale shadow of the real thing. But to Blotto's mind it was better than nothing.

*   *   *

April was early in the season for cricket, but the day was a beautiful one and as the game developed he felt his cares almost physically lifting off his shoulders. Even the prospect of being married to Mary Chapstick became a little less daunting. Once he was actually in the United States, he persuaded himself, introducing cricket couldn't really be that tricky, could it? And, as soon as they'd been shown the beauty of the sport, surely even Americans would very quickly make it their national game . . .? They wouldn't be able to resist, would they?

The natural setting of Blotto's emotional barometer pointed to 'Sunny'. It took a lot to change that. And when he was out hunting on Mephistopheles or playing cricket, nothing could affect his cheerful outlook on life. So his mood improved with the day.

The Semi-Colons may have been a scratch team of writers and poets, but they were no rabbits. Their ranks included three or four county players and one who'd even had a trial for England. Quality in the Tawcester Towers eleven was more variable. On the cricket pitch the Duke, Loofah, justified his second nickname. People who thought he was called 'Rupert the Unreliable' only because of his failure to impregnate his wife with a male heir hadn't observed his cricketing prowess. When batting he swung wildly at any ball that came his way. On the rare occasions when he made contact he was as likely to hit a boundary as to send the ball straight into a fielder's hands. Any ball he faced might just as easily be sent flying for six or return him to the pavilion.

But he was more skilled—and even more reliable—than most of the below stairs players. Though the Tawcester Towers chauffeur Corky Froggett knew the rudiments of the game, was a solid enough wicket keeper and played all right round the tail end of the batting order, the rest of the line-up was flimsy. Normally Blotto would bolster his team with some of his peers (who did actually happen to be peers), but again the Dowager Duchess hadn't wanted any people of their own status to meet the Chapsticks.

So really, given the quality in the rest of his team, the match was Blotto alone against the Semi-Colons.

Back on the veranda of the pavilion Twinks did her best to explain to Mary Chapstick the intricacies and subtleties of the game. It was an uphill struggle.

The American did understand the basic principle of tossing a coin to see which side batted first, but that was the extent of her comprehension. Once the game started, she got very lost indeed. Blotto, as captain of the Tawcester Towers team, had put the visitors in to bat and himself opened the bowling.

'What's he trying to do?' asked Mary Chapstick.

'He's trying to knock the two little horizontal bits of wood, which are called the "bails", off the three upright sticks, which are called the "stumps". And the whole thing's called the "wicket".'

'Well, that's easy if all he needs is to knock the bails off. He just has to give them a kick. They're right beside him.'

'No, he's aiming at the wicket the other end of the pitch.'

'Then why doesn't he get closer to it? That'd give him a better chance.'

'Because,' Twinks replied patiently, 'the laws of cricket state that the ball must be bowled from one end of the twenty-two-yard pitch to the other.'

'Why?' asked Mary Chapstick.

'Because that's what the laws of cricket say!'

'Gee, that's not very logical.'

Further discussion was interrupted by a ragged cry from the field of 'Howzat?' Blotto had taken the first wicket in his first over, neatly removing the opener's centre stump. Desultory applause accompanied the change of batsmen.

'What're they clapping for?' asked Mary Chapstick.

'Because Blotto's taken a wicket.'

'No, he hasn't.'

'Yes, he has.'

'Twinks, both the wickets are still there. He hasn't taken either of them.'

'The expression "taking a wicket" means . . .' But Blotto was once again taking his run-up. 'Let's just point the peepers at the game, shall we?'

'But it's difficult to watch it when I don't know what's going on,' said Mary Chapstick plaintively.

Twinks didn't respond. Blotto bowled the

remaining two balls of the over straight and true, but both were cautiously blocked by the new batsman (actually the one who'd had a trial for England). As the fielders changed sides there was another patter of applause from the pavilion.

'What're they clapping for this time?'

'Blotto's just bowled a maiden over.'

'That is certainly true,' said Mary Chapstick, blushing deeply.

'No, a maiden over is one in which no runs are scored. And in fact in this case it's even better, because Blotto bowled a wicket maiden.'

'I'm not wicked.'

'I didn't say you were. It's a wicket maiden because no runs were scored off the six balls and with one of those balls a wicket was taken.'

'Gee, it's a complicated game, isn't it? So Blotto's like the pitcher?'

'The bowler, we call it.'

'Like the hat?'

'Yes.'

'Well, why has he stopped being the hat?' Mary Chapstick pointed to the pitch, where a pimply underfootman was measuring out his run-up.

'Because you have to have someone different bowling from each end.'

'Why?'

'Because you just do!' Twinks foresaw that it was going to be a long afternoon.

The pattern for the game was now set. When Blotto was bowling, very few runs were allowed. When other members of the Tawcester Towers side took the ball, the Semi-Colons scored lavishly. At the end of the innings Blotto finished with the very respectable figures of ten wickets for the loss of only seven runs, but when facing the other Tawcester Towers bowlers, the opposition had notched up a score of 174.

He wasn't worried. As an opening batsman he knew what he had to do. Protect his less competent colleagues by ensuring that he faced as much of the Semi-Colons' bowling as possible. Though he managed his task very well, hitting sixes and fours and only running twos—or singles on the last ball of the over—he couldn't manage to keep the strike all the time. Slowly his team-mates' wickets fell to the usual mix of clean-bowled, caught and run out.

But Blotto remained quietly confident. There was only one wicket left to fall, but his partner was Corky Froggett who, though not an inspired cricketer, could be relied on not to make silly mistakes. The rest of the team, together with the usual no-balls and byes, had added seventeen runs, and Blotto was cruising along on 155. Three more runs to win. Three singles, except that would raise the potential risk of Corky facing the bowling. Better—and indeed classier and more stylish—for Blotto to win the game with a boundary.

But he didn't want to do anything rash. The Semi-Colon's bowler he was facing was the one who'd had the England trial and was no rabbit. Blotto blocked two balls that were targeted right on his middle stump, and waited for a looser delivery with which to achieve his boundary.

The next ball was a bit too loose. Far enough from Blotto's leg stump as almost to be a wide. He didn't even play a stroke at it; no sense in risking the game through impetuosity.

But as the ball whirred past him, Blotto heard sounds that were rare in his cricketing experience.

66

It was the clatter of the bails flying off the stumps behind him, followed by a ragged unison shout of 'Howzat?'

He turned in amazement to see the ruin of his wicket. Though by no logic that he knew could the ball have hit the stumps, Blotto still did the decent thing. It wasn't in his nature to argue with umpires. He shook Corky Froggett by the hand and walked back to the pavilion in a state of some bewilderment.

The Semi-Colons had won the match by two runs.

'What happened there?' Mary Chapstick asked Twinks.

'I've no idea. It's a bit of a rum baba. The ball didn't go anywhere near his stumps.'

'Then why's he coming back to the pavilion?'

'Because that's what Blotto's like, Mary. He's not the kind of stencher who'd argue with an umpire. He knows he wasn't really out, but he'd never admit that under threat of the thumbscrews. That's Blotto for you, I'm afraid.'

Mary Chapstick clasped her hands to her generous bosom. 'He is so wonderful,' she cooed. 'Who could fail to love a man who behaves like that?'

*   *   *

It was back in the pavilion that Corky brought him some kind of explanation for what had happened. The chauffeur had drawn the stumps and collected the bails at the end of the game. He held out one of the rounded wooden uprights to his master. 'Reckon that's what broke your wicket, milord.'

Blotto looked where Corky Froggett's stubby finger pointed. Embedded deep into the wood was a rifle bullet.

He took the evidence straight to his sister. Checking the bullet against the other in her reticule, the one that had killed Briscoe Daubeney-Vere, Twinks announced that both had been fired from the same rifle.

'Bit of an iffy Stilton, isn't it?' said Blotto. 'What kind of pot-brained pineapple would use that method to win a cricket match?'

'I don't think the cricket match had anything to do with it,' said Twinks. 'I think this bullet was meant for you, Blotters.'

'Toad-in-the-hole! But why? What could the stencher have against me?'

'I see a potential link of logic, Blotto me old frying-pan. I think I got things wrong. Mary Chapstick wasn't the target of the first bullet. The gunman shot the precise person he wanted to shoot.'

'Sorry? Not on the same page, Twinks me old ink-blotter.'

'I think Briscoe Daubeney-Vere was shot because he was perceived to be getting too chummy with Mary Chapstick, going out alone with her on to the terrace ...' She looked ominously at her brother. 'So you understand the implications of that, don't you?'

'No,' replied Blotto.

'You hardly spent a minute apart from Mary yesterday, did you? I think that made some lump of toadspawn jealous. He must have seen you together. He's already killed Briscoe Daubeney-Vere. And now he's out to kill you too.'

'Oh, broken biscuits,' said Blotto. This was a real gluepot, of a depth and viscosity unrivalled in previous gluepots. The mater was insistent that he should spend as much time as possible around Mary Chapstick. And yet if he did that he was liable to be shot ... even more than liable ... possibly even likely. Of course, there was no way he would have considered going against the mater's instructions. If the family honour required him to be shot, then shot he would be. It did seem a bit of a waste of a life, though.

9

The Ship of Sorrow

Blotto had never really seen the point of 'abroad'. Everything he required in life was available to him at Tawcester Towers. And though he'd met a few foreign boddos in his time, he couldn't really say that any of them had become close friends. He had a great respect for them, mind. They were generally speaking very good at hiding the inevitable disappointment that must have come with the realization that they hadn't been born British. Blotto knew that if he'd suffered that ghastly fate, he'd have spent all his time moaning on about it like a slapped puppy.

And if, on pain of death, he'd been forced to choose one bit of 'abroad' to go to, it certainly wouldn't have been America. Someone of Blotto's breeding had an instinctive suspicion of Republicanism. Having the toffs at the top was, in his view, the natural order of things. The feudal system had worked so well, Blotto often wondered why it had ever been abolished. In fact, the only thing he liked about America was some of the moving pictures it produced, and thanks to the invention of the cinematograph you didn't actually have to go to the place to enjoy those.

But he knew better than to imagine that he could cross the wishes of his mother. The Dowager Duchess had decreed that he was to travel to the United States to marry Mary Chapstick, and so that was what he had to do. He had once again turned optimistically to Twinks in the hopes that she might see some way out of his predicament, but unusually, having shot her bolt with the Duke of Godalming diversion, so far as other ideas were concerned she was an empty revolver.

During that summer, Blotto watched with appalled fascination as more and more details of his fate were settled. The weekend visit of Luther P. Chapstick III and his daughter to Tawcester Towers had been deemed, on both sides, a success. In the week that followed it, the Dowager Duchess's man of business had met up with the cattle baron and his attorney. After much wrangling, the basic terms for the financial aspect of Blotto and Mary's marriage had been agreed. The Dowager Duchess might be losing a son, but at least she had ensured the future of Tawcester Towers' plumbing.

Before he returned to the demands of meat-packing in the States, Luther P. Chapstick III had one final meeting with the Dowager Duchess at an hotel she favoured on her rare trips to London. There an end-of-November date was set for the wedding in Chicago. And a lot of time was devoted to discussion of the guest list. Magnanimously the Dowager Duchess agreed that the King and Queen of England, along with virtually every member of the House of Lords, would be enchanted to be invited and, for such a prestigious event, would undoubtedly clear their diaries to make the trip across the Pond. She suggested that, because of her patrician connections, the invitations, when printed, should be sent for distribution to her at Tawcester Towers (where of course, when they arrived, she would have them consigned to the nearest refuse receptacle). In spite of her assertions to the contrary, the Dowager Duchess had no intention of attending the wedding, nor of letting any of her aristocratic cronies even know that it was taking place.

So the Chapsticks took a luxury liner home. It was agreed that Blotto would follow the same route in November, arriving in Chicago a fortnight before the wedding. In the meantime, the affianced couple could write each other letters if they wished to. Mary Chapstick very definitely did wish to, and over the ensuing months many breathless avowals of love with transatlantic stamps on pink envelopes arrived at Tawcester Towers. Blotto, who had always been something of a slow reader, got halfway through the first one. And being an even slower writer, he didn't reply to any of them.

At their London meeting the Dowager Duchess had assured Luther P. Chapstick III that the engagement notice would be inserted in the Court Circular of *The Times*. With the printing set she had played with in the nursery Twinks created a reasonably good counterfeit version, which was duly sent off to Chicago. The Dowager Duchess still couldn't bring herself to risk any of her genuine aristocratic friends discovering that her son was committing the social gaffe of marrying an American.

Twinks had helped her mother out on that printing deception, but unwillingly. She was still desperately seeking an escape route for Blotto, but didn't want to alert the Dowager Duchess to this by any apparent lack of co-operation in the wedding plans.

Twinks did, however, insist that she should accompany Blotto on his wedding trip. There was a strong hereditary similarity between the two women and daughter could at times be as strong as mother. This was one of those occasions, and the Dowager Duchess, recognizing her equal, didn't argue but let Twinks have her way. Brother and sister would travel to Chicago together.

The summer passed for Blotto in a blur. Though he spent most of it playing his beloved cricket, he hardly noticed what he was doing. While centuries and wickets racked up with even greater frequency than usual, the only thought on his mind was that all of it was happening for the last time. The following summer he'd be incarcerated in America—watching rounders, for the love of strawberries!

Before the fated November day when he was due to board the SS *His Majesty*, Blotto did just manage to start the hunting season. But that experience too was soured for him. As he and the splendid Mephistopheles soared over hedge and gate and thicket, as foxes started thinking about wills and funeral arrangements, Blotto did not feel his customary surge of excitement. All he could think was, 'Never again, never again.'

Even Twinks could not pull off her usual trick of comforting him. When she bounced into a room, smiling her perfect smile, with a hearty cry of 'Larksissimo, Blotters me old bicycle pump!', the only reward from her brother was a wince of suffering.

She strained her magnificent brainbox in search of a solution to their dilemma, but atypically, nothing came.

*   *   *

For the passage from Southampton to New York brother and sister had adjoining staterooms on the SS *His Majesty*. It was a fine new liner on which every luxury taste was catered for. The cuisine was exceptional, the cellar magnificent. There was an extensive range of sporting activities laid on, and of course every pretty girl on board fell head over heels for Blotto. But none of this removed the furrow from his impossibly handsome brow. He traversed the decks with the expression of a man whose life imprisonment sentence has just been commuted to death.

He could not even share Twinks's amusement at the antics of Harvey. In the guise of the Dowager Duchess of Framlington, the Tawcester Towers housemaid was on the SS *His Majesty* with them. Somehow a personal wedding invitation to her from Luther P. Chapstick III had evaded the Dowager Duchess of Tawcester's censorship system. Given the offer, Harvey was not the kind to let a little detail like the illegitimacy of her title stop her from accepting. When informed of her plans, Grimshaw found his facial tic flickering like an early cinematograph film.

On board ship in her assumed role, Harvey behaved appallingly. With great relish and even greater insensitivity, she was rude to all the liner's staff unfortunate enough to come in contact with her. She wreaked a very personal revenge for all those years of slights from her betters. At times it seemed the very crassness of her insults would give away her subterfuge, but none of the SS *His Majesty*'s staff cottoned on. They'd seen far worse behaviour from genuine British aristocrats.

Whereas Blotto would normally have shared Twinks's glee at Harvey's disgraceful demeanour, nothing on that transatlantic trip could make him smile. Even going down to the hold, where his Lagonda was stored, and giving it a stroke, did not have its usual comforting effect. Nor did the old ritual of hugging his cricket bat before entering his bed for the night work its customary soothing magic.

Then, just when it seemed that nothing could make things worse, he received another body blow. He was sitting one evening over cocoa in Twinks's stateroom bemoaning his fate and saying, 'I think the only way I'm going to survive life in the States is by taking on copious draughts of the hard stuff. Maybe if I'm permanently wobbulated, I won't notice what a treacle tin I'm in.'

'Ah,' said Twinks.

His sister had quite an extensive repertoire of 'Ah's and Blotto recognized that this one didn't bode well. She had bad news to impart.

'What is it? Shift your shimmy. Come on, the rope's round my neck. Release the trapdoor.'

'It's about the hard stuff in the States, Blotto . . .'
'What about the hard stuff in the States?'
'There isn't any.'
'What!'
'You cannot purchase alcoholic beverages in the United States of America.'

'That can't be true. Come on, Twinks, you're jiggling my kneecap, aren't you? And I may say I take a pretty dim view of you making a joke out of something so important.'

'I am not joking, Blotto. On the twenty-eighth of October 1919 Congress passed the National Prohibition Act, better known as the Volstead Act, forbidding the sale and manufacture of alcohol.'

Blotto's lips opened and closed like those of a beached goldfish. The enormity of what he had just heard robbed him not only of speech but also of breath. He was in too advanced a state of shock even to say, 'Broken biscuits'. He'd known life in America was going to be bad, but it had never occurred to him that it might be that bad.

In fact there was only one event on that ship of sorrow which brought the slightest brightening to his mood. One evening when he was out on deck smoking a post-prandial cigar, he heard a loud report and felt something tug at his shoulder.

When the scene was examined by Twinks with the equipment from her reticule, she discovered a bullet-hole in the padding of her brother's dress coat. And from the wooden bulkhead in front of which he'd been standing, she used her penknife to extract a bullet.

A bullet from an Accrington-Murphy PL23 hunting rifle. Just like the one that had killed Briscoe Daubeney-Vere, alias the Duke of

Godalming. And the one that had been aimed at Blotto on the Tawcester Towers cricket field.

That discovery did bring a pale smile to her brother's careworn features. But not for a good reason. The fact that he was still the target for some crazed assassin cheered him by offering a means of escape from marriage to Mary Chapstick and a life without cricket or hunting.

Blotto was in a very bad way.

10

From Cattle to Can

The guided tour that Luther P. Chapstick III gave Blotto of the Chapstick Manufacturing Plant started at the top of a high tower, above which tall chimneys belted out thick, foul-smelling greasy smoke. His prospective father-in-law wore a tweed suit whose checks must have been designed by the makers of Battenburg cakes. Though it should have done, this garment totally failed to diminish the meat-packing magnate's enduring likeness to a warthog.

Chicago, Blotto had by now realized, was a city of very tall buildings, but the scene at their feet was low-rise, perhaps a square mile of stockyards from which arose a cacophony of confused lowing and a smell that was pure farmyard.

Blotto had been in the Land of the Free for less than a week and he was still adjusting to the strange habits of its citizens. So many things had surprised him—like the flamboyantly unnecessary height of their buildings, their obsession with iced water, their habits of driving on the wrong side of the road and saying 'gotten' when they should have said 'got'—that he had by then resolved not to be surprised by anything.

He had therefore made no comment when he and his host were greeted at the ostentatious gates of the Chapstick Manufacturing Plant (two giant statues of longhorns rearing up on either side) by a pair of thick-set gentlemen in double-breasted suits, each of whom was carrying a violin case. They were introduced as Jimmy 'The Moose' Fettuchini and Toni 'Nostrils' Linguini and they kept very close to Luther P. Chapstick III all the time he was on the premises. They did not speak at all, but let out growls of laughter every time their boss uttered anything that could be interpreted as a joke.

Blotto, trying without complete success to act like someone who wasn't surprised by anything, couldn't help himself from asking what the violins were for.

'You never know when you're going to need a little music,' Luther P. Chapstick III replied. This was clearly a joke, so far as Jimmy 'The Moose' Fettuchini and Toni 'Nostrils' Linguini were concerned, and was greeted by appropriate growls of laughter.

'Good ticket,' said Blotto. 'No, I suppose you don't ... when a boddo wants to do something impromptu ... you know, like that impromptu dance we had when you were staying at Tawcester Towers.'

'Oh, the music Jimmy 'The Moose' Fettuchini and Toni 'Nostrils' Linguini make ain't as upbeat as dance music.'

'Really?'

'It's more like the kinda music that puts people to sleep.'

This too was identified by the two men in double-breasted suits as a joke.

Luther P. Chapstick III led his guest to the guard-rail of the tower and pointed to the far end of the stockyards where there was a sizeable railway station. 'That's where they come in,' he said.

'Where who come in?'

'The cattle. The heifers, the steers. They're transported by trains from ranches way out west.'

The pause left after this suggested to Blotto that perhaps some response was required, so he offered a 'Hoopee-doopee!' Then, attempting to show an interest, he asked, 'So you buy the cattle from the boddos out there . . . the cowboys and cowgirls?' He'd seen enough moving pictures to reckon he'd got the terms right.

'No, Deveroox.' Luther P. Chapstick III had proved very resistant to the idea of his daughter marrying anyone called Blotto and insisted on using his proper name. Unfortunately, he had seen it written before hearing it spoken and, in spite of many attempts to correct him, insisted on pronouncing the final 'x'. 'That,' he went on, 'is how mollycoddled milksops do business.'

Blotto wasn't quite sure where the conversation was headed, so he just said, 'Good ticket.'

'I don't pay other folks to raise cattle so's I can buy from them. I raise the cattle myself.'

'What, here in Chicago?'

'I don't do the raising with my bare hands. I own the ranches, I own the cattle, I own the railroad, I own the stockyard.'

'Do you own Chicago too?' asked Blotto in

a tone that, for him, was almost acid. From the nursery onwards he had been taught that, if there was one thing that was really beyond the barbed wire, it was showing off. And since he'd arrived in America he'd heard rather more showing off than he would have wished to.

But the warthog's skin was impervious to such jibes. In fact, he took what had been said as a compliment. Slapping his prospective son-in-law on the shoulder, he roared, 'I like your style, Deveroox. No, I don't own Chicago yet, but that's only a matter of time . . . only a matter of time.'

This sally prompted growls of laughter from Jimmy 'The Moose' Fettuchini and Toni 'Nostrils' Linguini, but then there was another of those silences. Feeling he should fill it with something, this time Blotto opted for a 'Toad-in-the-hole.' This prompting no response, he looked down to the stockyards below and observed uncontroversially, 'That's a lot of cattle down there.'

'Sure is,' Luther P. Chapstick III agreed. 'And tomorrow this lot'll be gone and the pens'll be full again.'

'Erm . . . when you say "this lot'll be gone", what exactly do you mean?'

The meat-packing magnate clapped him on the shoulder. 'I will show you, Deveroox. I will show you exactly what I mean.'

*   *   *

Now Blotto could never really be described as squeamish. He was far too heroic and brave to give in to such weaknesses. Nor was he particularly sentimental about animals. Like any countryman of his class, much of the entertainment he enjoyed involved the wholesale slaughter of wild birds and mammals. But he still found the rest of that morning's guided tour of the Chapstick Manufacturing Plant challenging to the stability of his stomach.

His host, Luther P. Chapstick III, didn't understand the concept of self-effacement. Indeed his natural instinct was for self-aggrandisement. So everything that Blotto was shown that morning was not only the biggest in the world, but also the best in the world.

From their overview of the biggest stockyard in the world, Luther P. Chapstick III pointed out the alleyways that ran between the cattle pens, main thoroughfares in this city of beef. Along them men on horseback, armed with giant whips, would drive each newly released penful of livestock towards the grim complex of buildings at the end of the stockyards.

From the foot of the tower Blotto and his potential father-in-law (accompanied of course by Jimmy 'The Moose' Fettuchini and Toni 'Nostrils' Linguini) travelled to this complex in a small but luxuriously appointed railcar. There the guest was shown the broad ramps up which the cattle were driven and the chutes down which they slid and stumbled into the building.

Inside, Blotto was conducted on to a viewing gallery, surrounding a long room where the approaching drove of cattle were funnelled into a single metal-railed passageway, full of toiling men and bewildered lowing. As each animal reached the end of the queue, it was brained by a huge man with a sledgehammer. Then even while it staggered its last faltering steps, other men fixed to its legs chains that were attached to hooks on a giant metal wheel. As this turned, each dangling beast was lifted up off the ground before having its throat cut by another team of experts.

The carcasses were then detached from the wheel by more specialists and dropped down another chute to the floor below for further processes of skinning, scraping, beheading and eviscerating. Here again there was a team of experts for each noxious task. Their work was relentlessly repetitive, applying the same actions to each slab of meat, without pausing for a moment as the carcasses were endlessly replaced.

'Don't they get a bit bored, those boddos?' suggested Blotto as he looked down from the gallery. 'Pongling on at the same rombooley all day?'

'Who?' asked Luther P. Chapstick III.

'The men.'

'What men?' He genuinely didn't seem to know who Blotto was talking about.

'The workers. Don't they get bored?'

'They get paid. Who cares if they get bored?'

'Good ticket. I just wondered—'

'Well, don't wonder. I can do widdout a son-in-law who wonders.'

'Hoopee-doopee,' said Blotto in a conciliatory manner.

At the doorway through which the processed carcasses were moved on to the next procedure a bleary-looking man in a suit sat behind a desk. He was the first person in the plant who seemed to have nothing to do, so Blotto asked what his function was.

'He's the government inspector,' said Luther P. Chapstick III.

'So what does he do?'

'He checks the carcasses for disease.'

'But he doesn't seem to be doing anything.'

'No.' The meat-packing magnate roared with laughter and slapped Blotto heartily on the shoulders. 'Good, isn't it? We don't want to lose any of our precious beef to petty regulations, do we?'

Jimmy 'The Moose' Fettuchini and Toni 'Nostrils' Linguini thought that was funny too.

As they passed above the inspector, Blotto encountered the first promising thing since he had arrived in America. From the bleary-looking man emanated a strong smell of spirituous liquor. Maybe it *was* possible to get a drink in this godforsaken country.

The next cavernous room found a new crew of men working like automata. There the headless carcasses were split in half and further chopped up. Substantial parts of them were carted off for more refined butchering techniques, while the residue, unrecognizable chunks of flesh and organ mixed in with blood and sawdust from the floor, was tipped into the vast mouth of what Luther P. Chapstick III referred to as 'The Great Grinder', from whose splattered interior a ghastly crunching of cogs sounded.

A little unwillingly, Blotto found himself asking in which product of the Chapstick range those particular remnants ended up.

'They go into our Beef Extract,' his host replied. 'Mixed in nourishing soups and drinks and spread on toast at breakfast tables all over the US of A.'

82

The rest of the guided tour encompassed pickling rooms, salting rooms and smoking rooms (though not of the genteel kind Blotto was used to in his London club). He saw carcasses hung in huge refrigerators and even in refrigerated trains. He witnessed the construction of crates and cans. He saw machines sticking on brightly coloured labels for Chapstick's Canned Beef, Chapstick's Corned Beef, Chapstick's Dressed Beef, Chapstick's Beef Sausages and a thousand other beef-derived products.

Blotto also saw what was done with the less edible remains, the ones that had escaped even The Great Grinder. The hides were taken to the on-site tanneries. The fats were turned into lard and soap, intestines used to case sausages, hoofs melted down into glue. Even the horns were transformed into combs and buttons. All the processes witnessed that morning seemed to bear out Luther P. Chapstick III's assertion that: 'We use every bit of the animal except the moo.'

The tour finished in the same building where it had started, but on a lower floor, in a lavish boardroom. This too gave a splendid view over the expanses of the Chapstick beef empire. As they stood side by side at the window, his host clapped a hearty arm on the younger man's shoulder. 'Treat my Mary right, Deveroox,' he said, 'and one day all this could be yours.'

Blotto couldn't find words to express his reaction. The Tawcester family had been involved in some pretty unsavoury businesses over the years—not excluding the slave trade— but meat-packing ... A shudder ran through his godlike frame.

Needless to say, Luther P. Chapstick III misinterpreted this reaction. 'I can understand you're dumbstruck, my boy, at how wonderful it all is, but you'll get used to the idea. And now . . .' he clapped his hands 'Lunch!'

At the signal, Jimmy 'The Moose' Fettuchini and Toni 'Nostrils' Linguini took up position on either side of the door with their violin cases at the ready (almost like soldiers on sentry duty, thought Blotto), and the boardroom was suddenly full of uniformed waiters. Blotto and Chapstick sat at opposite ends of the huge table on which fine linen and silver cutlery appeared as if by magic. To Blotto's disappointment, the only liquid on offer was iced water. In the middle of the table was placed a salver on which were displayed three plates and a bowl of lettuce, tomatoes, cucumber and coleslaw. On a silver stand at the centre stood a can of Chapstick's Corned Beef.

Ceremoniously the can was opened by the head waiter. He let the gelatinous slab slide down on to one of the plates, then carved it with all the respect that would have been accorded to a Thanksgiving turkey. He placed two slices on each of the plates, garnished them with the cold vegetables and ordered lesser waiters to place them in front of the two diners.

'After what you've seen this morning,' said Luther P. Chapstick III, 'I'm sure you're gonna wanna taste some of the Chapstick goodies.'

Blotto looked down at his plate and felt the bile rising in his throat.

'I'm frightfully sorry. You must excuse me,' he managed to utter as he dashed past Jimmy 'The Moose' Fettuchini and Toni 'Nostrils' Linguini and

84

out of the room.

But then Blotto had never liked salad.

11

A Heart to Heart for the Engaged Couple

Blotto and Twinks thought that calling the mansion Chapstick Towers was a bit of a liberty. Granted, the place did have towers, but then it had every other feature that the imagination of architects had devised over the centuries. Palladian columns, Assyrian reliefs, Tudor beamed frontages, Rhine castle turrets, cathedral-scale vaulted ceilings, ecclesiastical stained glass, nothing had been omitted in the construction of Luther P. Chapstick III's home, set in a thousand acres of land on the shores of Lake Michigan. Nothing, that is, except for taste.

The thing that Blotto and Twinks found rather pitiful was the way their host kept going on about how *old* everything was. They realized that no one in America really understood the word. No building in the entire country had been around for more than 400 years, for the love of strawberries! And most of the structures they saw had been created in the last fifty. Chapstick Towers had only been started in the previous decade, following its owner's specifications, and it was still in many ways a work in progress. Luther P. Chapstick III was clearly capable of adding any number of new features to it, as his familiarity with foreign architecture increased. During his recent visit to London, he had been mightily impressed by Marble Arch and was proposing to build a full-size replica for the main entrance to his estate.

What he seemed unable to understand, though Blotto and Twinks very patiently tried to explain it to him, was that using old materials in a building did not make the building itself old. Luther P. Chapstick III kept boasting about the antiquity of the architectural features he had sourced in Europe and had rebuilt brick by brick on his estate. The fact that the Elizabethan chimneys came from a genuine English stately home, or that the rose window in the dining room had once graced a German cathedral did not impart the dignity of history to the new edifice on to which they had been grafted.

Another detail that distinguished Chapstick Towers from a genuine English stately home was the fact that everything inside the place was so aggressively clean. People of Blotto and Twinks's background knew instinctively that the patina of good furniture was dust. In just the same way that the leadpenny aristocrats who had been set up at Tawcester Towers for the Chapsticks' visit had looked too smart and needed to wear clothes that had been scruffied up a bit, so Chapstick Towers looked far too pristine to pass muster.

The mansion had other features that showed it not to be the genuine article. The plumbing, for instance, was not only efficient but also silent. Many of the bedrooms actually had en suite bathrooms which featured showers. (Blotto reacted against such abominations; knew from birth that the only proper place for a shower was in the changing room after a sporting encounter.) Also some kind of central heating system kept the entire interior of Chapstick Towers at a constantly pleasant temperature. And everyone who knew anything knew that you couldn't have a genuine stately home without draughts.

So Blotto and Twinks, though far too polite to let anyone guess their feelings, were distinctly unimpressed by their host's home. The thought that he might have to spend the rest of his life there appalled Blotto. And the thought of all the fine hunting in England that he was missing that November caused him a constant pain, like an abscess on a tooth.

His mood was not improved by the fact that all Mary Chapstick could talk about in his presence (or indeed anyone else's) were plans for their wedding. And references to things she'd written in her letters to him (which of course he hadn't read).

*　　　*　　　*

Blotto tried to escape the onslaught by keeping out of her way as much as possible. The scale on which Chapstick Towers had been built made it possible to find lots of out-of-the-way wings in which to hide. The trouble was, though, that having watched the mansion virtually grow up around her, Mary knew its geography very well and there was nowhere he could remain undiscovered for long.

One afternoon he was looking moodily out of a window which had once graced the frontage of a Venetian *palazzo* and entertaining most unBlottolike thoughts. His mood was down because, although he wasn't actually dependent on the stuff, he would at that moment have sold the family silver for a drop of alcohol. Just a brandy and soda . . . with maybe the bottle and siphon left beside him for a few top-ups. But so far the only evidence he'd encountered of alcohol in the United States had been the whiff on the breath of the inspector in the meat-packing plant. He certainly hadn't been offered even a small sherry since his arrival at Chapstick Towers.

Maybe the lack of alcoholic comfort was the reason for his uncharacteristic thoughts. In spite of his strong in-built sense of honour, he was actually contemplating ducking out of the current obligation. Suppose he just upped and left Chapstick Towers . . . drove down to New York in the Lagonda and caught the first ship back to England . . .? What was the worst that could happen?

The image of his mother rose fully formed in his brain, and he knew immediately what was the worst that could happen.

This gloomy reverie was interrupted by the appearance of Mary Chapstick, who had once again discovered his hide-out. She was, as ever, looking the complete breathsapper in a tiny dress of violet silk. No doubt about it, Mary was a spoffingly fine piece of womanflesh. The boddo who got her as his bride would really have won the raffle. Just so long as that boddo wasn't Blotto.

Feeling guilty about his unworthy yearnings for escape, he still thought it was worth seeing whether he could find a chink in the armour of her certainty that she wanted to marry him.

'Mary me old cushion-cover . . .' he began.

'Yes, Blotto?' she responded, with a look in her eyes that did look ominously like love.

'Hasn't it ever occurred to you that you could

have a better chance in the old matrimonial stakes if you'd saddled up a different donkey?'

'No, Blotto. It's never occurred to me. Not since I've met you.'

Was there a little chinkette in what she'd just said? Worth probing. 'Not since you've met me?' he echoed. 'Are you suggesting that, before you clapped your peepers on me, you were looking for something different?'

'Well, of course I was, Blotto.' That was promising. 'Before I met you I didn't know I was going to meet you, did I? I didn't know that I was about to meet the love of my life.' That was less promising.

'But,' Blotto persisted, 'when you were younger, wasn't there some other poor thimble on whom you'd set your beadies? Didn't you have a childhood sweetheart?'

'Well, there was someone . . .'

Promising again. 'Toad-in-the-hole,' said Blotto. 'And who was the lucky pineapple in question?'

'His name was Sophocles Katzenjammer.' As she said the words an encouragingly misty look came into her eyes.

'And what you felt for this poor old greengage was real love, was it?'

'I thought so at the time,' Mary replied, again raising Blotto's hopes. Before dashing them again by continuing, 'But that was before I'd met you and found out what real love is.'

Blotto had another go. 'I suppose it's possible,' he said, 'that if you met this Sophocles Katzenwhatever again, you might find the old embers of love rekindling a bit . . . even flickering up into a spoffing great conflagration . . . don't you

89

think . . .?'

'No,' Mary disagreed forcefully. 'Not after the way he treated me.'

'Why? What did the stencher do?'

'He pretended he loved me. He said he wanted to marry me. But of course my father would never have consented to the marriage.'

'Why's that?'

'Because Sophocles Katzenjammer was a Katzenjammer.'

'Sorry? Not on the same page. Are the Katzenjammers some kind of religious sect?'

'No. Sophocles was a Katzenjammer of the Katzenjammer Beef Extract family.'

'Ah, rival business to your pater's?'

'You can say that again. The rivalry between Chapstick's and Katzenjammer's makes the Great War look like a kindergarten scuffle. There's no way my pop would let me marry a Katzenjammer.'

'But some young droplets when they've been in love,' suggested Blotto, 'have found parental opposition made them even keener to twiddle up the old reef-knot. Happens in some play of Shakespeare's, I seem to recall. Called "Somebody and" . . . er, "Somebody" . . . An example of a family feud turning up the toaster of love.'

'That was how I reacted with Sophocles at first,' Mary Chapstick admitted. 'I said I'd marry him in spite of my pop. To spite my pop, in fact. I agreed to elope with him. We were going to go to Florida to get married.'

'Buzzbanger of an idea,' said Blotto. 'So what went wrong?'

'I was waiting for him at the barrier of Chicago Union Station on the night when we'd agreed to run away together ...' The memory was still painful; it brought a tremble to her lower lip '... and he never showed up—the two-faced coyote!'

'Tough Gorgonzola,' Blotto sympathized. 'Maybe this Sophocles pineapple got delayed, or ... I mean surely you can forgive a boddo for—'

'No woman can ever forgive being stood up!' asserted Mary, sounding for the first time unnervingly like her father. Which really put the candle-snuffer on Blotto's thoughts of catching the next ship back home. It just wasn't in his nature to behave like that kind of toadspawn.

'He probably had some perfectly reasonable explanation,' he struggled on hopelessly. 'Next time you see him, you might suddenly realize you'd just got your mitten-strings tangled, and the flipmadoodles might drop off your eyes and you might realize that you love the old pongler after all.'

'That could never happen,' said Mary Chapstick.

'Why ever not?'

'Because since I last saw Sophocles Katzenjammer, I have met you. And now I know what real love is.'

Blotto squirmed inwardly. And he would have to squirm a lot more—inwardly and outwardly—if he was going to get off this particular hook.

12

Wedding Plans

The Chainey Hotel in Chicago was new and big—really big. Too big, to Blotto's mind. What was the point of a building having so many floors, except to give a boddo neck-ache? Come to that, what was the point of even having a hotel in a country that didn't serve alcohol?

The night when Luther P. Chapstick III took his prospective son-in-law to the Chainey, he acted like he owned the place. Though Blotto was getting used to the cattle baron's habit of acting like he owned everywhere, he still couldn't help asking, 'Do you actually own this?'

Chapstick thought the question was funny, funny enough to justify a hearty laugh and a resounding slap on the younger man's shoulders. 'I don't exactly own it,' he replied, 'but let's say I have an understanding with the management.'

He chuckled and nodded acknowledgement to two dark-jowled men with violin cases who stood in the hotel's enormous crystal-encrusted lobby. When Blotto looked around he saw more and more men with violin cases, all eyeing each other suspiciously.

'Lot of musician boddos in Chicago, aren't there?' observed Blotto. 'Is there some kind of big concert coming up?'

'In Chicago,' said Luther P. Chapstick III, again chuckling, 'there's a big concert every night. The violin cases get opened and the evening always ends in fireworks.'

'Hoopee-doopee.'

'Now listen, Deveroox, I said we'd come here this evening to check on the catering arrangements for Mary-Bob's wedding.' Increasingly that was how her father referred to the forthcoming celebration. The identity of the man she was marrying had become an irrelevance. Blotto in fact didn't mind this. It comforted him, offering him a momentary hope that nobody might notice if he wasn't actually present at the ceremony. He knew that sadly it wasn't true, but he enjoyed the illusion.

'But as it happens,' Chapstick went on, 'I have other business to conduct in the hotel tonight, so I'll get one of the staff to show you the doings.' He stopped a passing flunkey in a smart suit. 'Get the Catering Manager!'

'Of course, sir. Who shall I say wants him?'

'Tell him it's about the Chapstick wedding. And he'll be meeting a very important guest from abroad, to whom he should supply everything he asks for. The boofer in question is Lord Deveroox Lyminster.'

'I'm not actually a lord, to be correct, in—'

'Lip it!' snapped his prospective father-in-law. Then, seeming to lose interest, he moved away. 'When you're through, get a cab back to Chapstick Towers. I'll see you in the morning.' He crossed to the reception counter.

And there, except that it was so unlikely that Blotto knew it couldn't be true, he could have sworn he heard Luther P. Chapstick III ask whether the Dowager Duchess of Framlington was in her room and expecting him.

*   *   *

93

Though the Chainey's Catering Manager was dressed in immaculate tails, he had the thick-set body and dark jowls of Jimmy 'The Moose' Fettuchini and Toni 'Nostrils' Linguini ... and indeed many of the other gentlemen in the hotel lobby. All he lacked was a violin case. Instead, under his arm he carried a folder tasselled with silver silk.

He shook Blotto's hand as though he were trying to squeeze all the juice out of a grapefruit. 'Great to meet you, Duke.'

'I'm not actually a duke. I'm—'

'Never mind that, Earl.'

'Nor am I actually—'

'Who cares? You're a member of the British aristocracy.'

'Yes, I am, but—'

'And hey, I hear congratulations are in order. You gonna marry old Chapstick's daughter. That'd be good news for anyone. The guy who gets that dame is also gonna get one helluva lotta beef.'

'So I gather,' said Blotto, for whom the attractions of beef were quickly waning.

'Like I say,' the Catering Manager went on, 'you two getting hitched is good news. Chicago could do with a bit of class.'

For the first time since his arrival in the United States, Blotto found himself agreeing with something that had been said.

'Let me show you the Banqueting Suite,' said the Catering Manager, leading him to a crystal-encrusted door at the far end of the lobby. 'And I can assure you, Duke—'

'I'm not actually a duke ...' Oh, what was the

94

point? Blotto gave up.

'I can assure you that security in the Chainey is always very tight. You won't have no worries about that on your wedding day.'

'Why should I worry about—?'

'We check everything out. The Boss insists on that. We even check out the inside of the wedding cake.'

'But what on earth could be inside—?'

'Dwarf with a Tommy gun. Has been known. But we find a dwarf in your wedding cake, don't worry, he'll be taken for a ride before it gets to the table. That's all part of the service here at the Chainey.'

'Good ticket,' said Blotto, unwilling to admit to being slightly confused.

The Banqueting Hall that they had just entered was an exact replica of the Galerie des Glaces at the Palace of Versailles. Lights twinkling from the many chandeliers were reflected back by the high mirrors. Blotto could not fail to be impressed by the sight.

'Not a bad little chicken coop for a wedding reception,' said the Catering Manager. 'Kinda place you're going to remember for the happiest day of your life, wouldn'tcha say?'

Blotto was struck dumb, appalled by the thought that the next time he entered this room it would be as a married man. 'Happiest day of his life' . . . what a ghastly gluepot. Oh, biscuits shattered into an infinite number of pieces!

'Now, Duke . . .' The Catering Manager opened his elaborate tasselled silver folder and produced an elaborate tasselled sheet of fine card. 'I have here some menu suggestions from our chef, Monsewer Dewboyes, who is French. Maybe you

95

would like to take them home to discuss with your betrothed?'

Blotto, thinking it very unlikely that he'd be able to eat anything at the reception, wordlessly took the menus.

Another tasselled object was drawn from the folder. 'And here is the wine list. If I know Mr Chapstick, I'm sure he will only want the best champagne, but maybe that's another thing you and your betrothed would like to discuss.'

It took a moment for Blotto to take in what he was hearing, but then, in the voice of a man who has just crawled thirstily for two weeks across the Sahara, he echoed the one word: 'Champagne?'

'Sure.'

'But ...' Blotto went on, still hardly able to believe his ears, 'I thought the sale of all wobbulators was prohibited in the United States.'

'Yeah, but ...' The Catering Manager shrugged his heavy shoulders evocatively. 'Listen, the Boss has ways of managing these things. And when the host of the party's Luther P. Chapstick III ... Besides, the Police Chief and his mob are all going to be guests at the wedding—they'd be real soured up if they didn't get their hooch.'

The implication of these words was so wonderful that Blotto was still tentative about accepting it. 'You mean it is possible to get a drink in this country ...?'

The Catering Manager chuckled. 'Everything can be fixed if you know the right people. And the Boss sure is the right people.'

'Would it be possible,' asked Blotto, still scared that the Saharan oasis forming in his mind might be a mirage, 'for me to get a drink right now?'

Another chuckle, and Blotto was rewarded with the most welcome word he'd heard since his arrival in the United States. 'Sure.'

13

Twinks Alone

It was rare that the barometers of the two younger Lyminster siblings were set to 'Cloudy'. Like Blotto's, Twinks's customary disposition was a sunny one. So long as Blotto had uninterrupted access to his hunting and his cricket, he thought life by and large was a pretty good ticket. Twinks too generally found that most situations were 'Larksissimo!' And on the rare occasion when either experienced some kind of setback, the other could normally be relied on to provide adequate jollying up and bolstering until the benign status quo was restored.

But that process of mutual regulation was not happening during their stay at Chapstick Towers. The cause of Blotto's disquiet was too obvious to need spelling out, but Twinks was also uncharacteristically subdued. Part of the reason for this came from witnessing her brother's unhappiness. It hurt her almost physically to see him so crabwhacked.

But, even more than that, she felt Blotto's condition reflected her own inadequacy. Twinks was acknowledged as the family brainbox. However dire the situation, she could normally be relied on to negotiate a way out of the treacle tin. And yet here she was, with her brother closer to the precipice of matrimony than he'd ever been, and she was proving to be an empty revolver.

She racked her brains, but they proved stubbornly resistant to racking. She even sought outside assistance. At St Raphael's College, Oxford, resided the one person in the world whose intellect was possibly even more powerful than her own, Professor Erasmus Holofernes. Because of the long delay in response to a ship-borne letter and the unavailability of transatlantic telephone services, she had sent him a cablegram, outlining their current predicament, but the professor had been uncharacteristically slow in replying. So there was no immediate help from that quarter.

Twinks tried to distract herself with her usual resources. These included leading a wild social life, but that didn't seem to be on offer at Chapstick Towers. True, she had been introduced to a lot of Mary's friends, but the vapid girls only seemed interested in the forthcoming wedding, and as for the young men . . . well, it was the usual thing. With deadening predictability they all fell in love with her, which Twinks found extremely tiresome. She kept swatting them off like so many mosquitoes.

There were of course other things she could do to occupy her mind. In rare moments of accidie she had frequently resorted to translation. For this trip she had brought with her from Tawcester Towers a copy of Montaigne's *Essais* and had made a start on a Japanese version of that, but it didn't seem to have engaged her mind as forcibly as such diversions usually did. She felt restless and dissatisfied with herself.

And she knew she would go on feeling that way until she had somehow managed to get Blotto out of the proposed marriage to Mary Chapstick. Only when the pair of them had returned permanently to Tawcester Towers would she feel any sense of serenity.

The trouble was that every time she brought her mind to bear on the problem, she was faced with the same unalterable facts. The usual reason for the cancellation of nuptials was sudden cold feet on behalf of one or other of the proposed participants. Well, Mary was very definitely a non-starter so far as that was concerned. Her feet—and indeed every other part of her—seemed to be permanently on the toasting fork.

And while Blotto's feet could have been used very effectively to chill a whole cellarful of white wine, this wasn't a new condition. He'd felt like that from the first moment the marriage had been suggested. But his innate sense of family honour—not to mention a healthy respect for the will of his mother—meant there was no question of his backing out voluntarily.

Of course, engagements had been broken off many times because of the infidelity of one or other of the parties involved, usually the man. If the affianced boddo were to go off and have a rampant public affair, ideally with a woman no better than she should be ... well, the cancellation notices would soon be in the post.

But Twinks only very briefly entertained that idea. She was dealing with Blotto after all, and her brother's general ineptitude about encounters with the opposite sex made it difficult to put his name in the same sentence as the words 'rampant public affair'.

Another cause for the ending of an engagement

could be the sudden realization on the part of one or other parent that the union was unsuitable for reasons of breeding, imbecility or criminality. But here again no change was likely to occur. The Dowager Duchess had known from the start that the Chapsticks were unsuitable—they were *Americans*, for the love of strawberries!—but she didn't let that interfere with her plans. The financial security of Tawcester Towers—not to mention its plumbing—was more important than such social considerations. And if a younger son had to be sacrificed to achieve that end … well, worse things had happened to the Lyminsters during the Crusades.

The evening that Blotto had accompanied Luther P. Chapstick III to the Chainey Hotel Twinks had been left alone at Chapstick Towers (alone, that is, except for the army of servants and bodyguards who peopled the place, but of course someone of her breeding didn't notice them). Mary had gone off to dine with her bridesmaids and, although Twinks had been invited, she'd refused the invitation. Too gracious to say that she was actually fed up to the back teeth with talk of the wedding, she'd pleaded the excuse of a headache. But in fact she did have plans for the evening.

Blotto had reported to her the details of his latest heart to heart conversation with his fiancée and from it Twinks had extracted one tiny scrap of hope—Mary's mention of her previous admirer, Sophocles Katzenjammer. The feud between Luther P. Chapstick III and the Katzenjammers was clearly a ferocious one. If Blotto could somehow be manoeuvred into an alliance—or the appearance of an alliance—with the Katzenjammers … if he could perhaps just be caught with the smell of Katzenjammer Beef Extract on his breath . . . well, Mary's father might suddenly feel very differently about allying his daughter to such a debased character.

Twinks had only the one thread of thought to weave into the tapestry of a plan, but she didn't have anything else. And the situation was so desperate that she had to start somewhere.

So, abandoning her Japanese translation in the middle of Montaigne's *Essai* 'To philosophize is to learn how to die', and picking up her sequinned reticule, she left her room and set out to explore Chapstick Towers.

*   *   *

By now Twinks knew her way around the sprawling pile and she had no doubt about her initial destination. At the front of the house was a room whose interior was that of a hunting lodge transported from the grounds of an Austrian *Schloss*, which Luther P. Chapstick III used as his study. Previous casual exploration had revealed to Twinks that he always kept the door locked. But after checking round the hall (reassembled from a Maharajah's palace in Lahore) to see that she was unobserved, it took a matter of moments for her to use the picklocks in her reticule to gain entrance.

Once inside, she relocked the door, reasoning that if any passing servant or bodyguard tried it, they would then find nothing untoward. The heavy curtains were drawn, so she had no anxiety about switching on the electric lights. Though she had not been in the room before, she went instinctively to the large desk, which had once belonged to Pope Gregory XIII and was set in a window bay which in daytime commanded unrivalled views over Lake Michigan.

The sixteenth-century Italian locksmiths had been clever, but not clever enough to thwart the contents of Twinks's reticule. Within seconds she had Luther P. Chapstick III's desk open. She didn't know exactly what she was looking for, but at least for the first time since she'd arrived in the United States, Twinks felt she was doing something useful. The familiar thrill prompted by a new investigation ran through her slender body.

She had been vaguely hoping to find some details of the past history between the Chapsticks and the Katzenjammers, but what the desk offered was something infinitely more valuable. Something that Twinks reckoned could offer the very real prospect of getting Blotto out of his engagement to Mary Chapstick.

So excited was she by her discovery that, when she slipped out of the study on the way back to her bedroom, she did not notice that her movements were observed from the shadows in the hall by Jimmy 'The Moose' Fettuchini.

14

At Last—a Drink!

Blotto had expected that the Chainey Hotel Catering Manager would take him straight to one of the many bars around the lobby and provide him with alcohol, but he was informed that all he could get there would be soft drinks, teas, lemonades and other of the noxious sugary concoctions that he had been served at Chapstick Towers. The route to a real drink proved to be far more circuitous.

The Catering Manager led him through the hotel's kitchens and out into a seedy, minimally lit street behind. Next to the closed metal shutter of a run-down garage was a small, rusting metal door. A mean single bulb shed a grudging light on dirty uncarpeted stairs. The Catering Manager nodded his head for Blotto to follow him down them.

The light hardly reached the next door at the foot of the stairs. Blotto could just see the outline of the Catering Manager's arm raised and the knuckles tapping a rhythmic tattoo on the dull metal. There was a silence, then a circle of light appeared as a peephole was uncovered. The light was quickly blocked and the glitter of a single eye could be seen at the aperture.

'*Ciao*,' said the Catering Manager. '*Issa Giuseppe.*'

The double doors provided very effective soundproofing and, as Blotto was ushered through the second one and the thick curtain that hung on its inside, his ears were suddenly assailed with noise. As his eyes accommodated to the dusky interior, he became aware of a band of coloured musicians over the far side of the room, jumping about vigorously to the hectic beat. Though Twinks was an aficionado of jazz, Blotto had had little experience of the new sound. And the little he'd had, had come courtesy of gramophone records. He'd never heard a live jazz band before.

Nor had he seen a live jazz singer. The musicians were fronted by a woman of exceptional, insolent beauty. She wasn't young, probably only just hanging on to her thirties, but that augmented rather than diminished her attractions. She was dressed completely in black, a small shimmering black dress which failed to reach her black silk-stockinged knees. Black shoes with a high heel and straps across the front. About her neck hung long loops of threaded jet. The whiteness of her bare arms and face provided a sharp monochrome contrast. Her eyes were a dark, smoky blue.

But the glory of her was the splash of colour provided by her hair, which was a deep, lustrous red, cut in the contemporary style like an acorn cup. And equally impressive was the voice that issued from her painted red lips, as she sang:

I've always been mistreated,
Beaten up and cheated.
My man he treats me cruel,
Plays me for a fool,
But when I walk out the door,
I soon come back for more,
Though he's more interested in the booze.
That's why I'm singing . . .
The . . .

Kept in my place, slapped in the face,
Worried around, knocked to the ground . . .
Pick myself up again blues.

The voice had been long marinated in gin and smoke, and it had a strange effect on Blotto. Although he was generally inept in social exchanges with the opposite sex, here was a communication that cut out the awkward necessity of conversation. It seemed to slice through to some deep core of his being and left him strangely stirred. He didn't know how to describe the voice, but then he had not yet encountered the relatively new word 'sexy'.

He stood frozen in the doorway, mesmerized by the singer's looks and voice, and the Catering Manager had to shake him back to normal functioning. 'Duke, you said you wanted a drink . . .'

'Oh yes, yes I do,' Blotto agreed. And as he dragged his eyes reluctantly away from the chanteuse, he became aware of a very welcome sight. On all of the tables in the crowded space stood bottles, all the customers had glasses in their hands, and the smoky air was loaded with the tang of alcohol. A lot of violin cases lay beside their owners' chairs. At one table all of the customers were dressed in police uniforms, and they seemed to be carousing with even more enthusiasm than the rest of the crowd.

'Then you better come and meet the Boss,' said the Catering Manager, leading Blotto across to a table near the stage.

There was no doubt which of the men he was referring to. Though all of them were dressed in similar double-breasted suits, all had similar thick-set bodies and heavy jowls, there was one to whom the body angles of all the others deferred. His face was diagonally bisected by a scar in three sections, a line across the forehead losing itself in a bushy eyebrow, continuing across the broken nose and ending with a final oblique on the cheek. The man was very still—more facial expression had frequently been observed in paving slabs—but nothing escaped the scrutiny of his cold, reptilian eyes.

'Boss,' said the Catering Manager. 'I'd like to introduce you to the Duke of Lyminster Deveroox.' Blotto had long given up hope of Americans getting his title right, but he still winced at having the final 'x' of his Christian name sounded.

The 'Boss' very slowly raised his eyes to the newcomer, appraised him for a moment, then gestured to the empty seat beside him. 'Join me,' he said. 'I'm Mr Chiaparelli.'

'Known as Spagsy,' added one of the heavies in a voice that suggested he'd been on the booze for a while.

The Boss's glacial eyes flicked across to look at the man. 'Did I hear myself giving you permission to call me Spagsy?' he asked in a quiet, level voice.

'No, Boss, I just—'

'Nobody calls me Spagsy without my permission.'

In a smooth quick movement, he drew a small revolver out of a shoulder holster inside his pinstriped jacket and shot the offending man.

'People gotta have respect,' said Spagsy Chiaparelli. 'Otherwise civilization goes out the window.'

'I'm sorry,' said Blotto, who felt he couldn't let the killing he'd just witnessed go completely unremarked, 'but did you shoot that boddo simply because he called you . . .?' He teetered on the edge of saying 'Spagsy' but, remembering the reaction such a lapse had just prompted, thought better of it '. . . because he didn't use the proper form of address to you?'

'Hell, whadda you take me for?' demanded the Boss, his hands innocently outstretched. 'Some kinda hoodlum? The reason I shot that chimp was because he's a multiple murderer.'

'Toad-in-the-hole!'

'With my own eyes I seen him shoot down fourteen men in cold blood.' He appealed to the other men at the table for corroboration. 'That scumdouche killed fourteen men, didn't he?'

'Twenty-three,' asserted one of the heavies. 'But you weren't there for all of them, Mr Chiaparelli.'

'See?' Again the Boss opened his hands out to Blotto. 'Any dingle who takes twenty-three innocent boofers for a ride, he deserves the death penalty, doesn't he?'

'Well, maybe, but—'

'So that's what I give him, wannit?'

'Maybe. Technically, though, I think a death penalty should only be given after a due process of law.'

'A due process of law? You mean a trial, do you, Duke?'

'Yes, I suppose—'

'And what happens at a trial? A bunch of witnesses say they saw the fligger commit the crime, he's found guilty—death penalty—bang! Same due process as what you just saw here.'

'It's still not exactly how these things're done in England.'

107

'Hey, we're not in England now, are we? Here we're in a new country. Here we just do things quicker is all.' The impassive features were turned on Blotto with the tiniest flicker of surprise. 'You weren't thinking I was one of the bad guys, were you? I'm on the side of good. I wouldn't shoot nobody except in the cause of justice. Look!' He pointed to the group of men who were removing the body. 'If I was a bad guy, would the police be helping with that?'

It was a very good point, thought Blotto. Three uniformed policemen were part of the corpse-carrying team. He felt rather guilty for the unworthy suspicions he'd had of Spagsy Chiaparelli. Other countries had different ways of doing things. Of course they weren't right—only the British could always be relied on to do the right thing—but one had to respect their customs. He nodded to the Boss and said, 'Good ticket.'

Spagsy graciously acknowledged the apology before saying, 'You'll be wanting a drink.'

'You can say that again,' agreed Blotto, who was still feeling a little confused. Although he had now accepted the full explanation for what had happened, he wasn't sure of the correct etiquette to be followed when your host has just shot someone.

'What you drink then, Duke?'

Blotto had been waiting so long to be asked that question that he had a momentary doubt as to what to answer. 'Erm, what do you have?'

'Everything.'

The memory came to Blotto of a particularly brain-rearranging cocktail that he'd been introduced to at the Savoy Hotel in London. 'It wouldn't be possible to organize a St Louis

Steamhammer, would it, Mr Chiaparelli?' Recent experience had made him careful to get the correct mode of address.

'Sure.' Spagsy Chiaparelli snapped his fingers. A waiter materialized instantly beside him and one of his acolytes gave the drink order.

There was a silence . . . well, a silence except for the jazz band, the sultry singing of the chanteuse and the raucous chat from all the other tables.

Feeling he should perhaps break it, Blotto said, 'This is beezer, isn't it?' Then, after no one reacted, he continued, 'Certainly lighting the fireworks of fun here, aren't we?'

Still silence. Blotto wasn't usually very perceptive, but on this occasion he intuited that there was a rule at the table where he was sitting. No one initiated a conversation except for Spagsy Chiaparelli. If he didn't say anything, then there was silence. Blotto stayed silent until his St Louis Steamhammer arrived.

Oh, the bliss of that first taste, the burning of the alcohol against the roof of his mouth. It wasn't much more than a week since he'd had his last proper drink on the SS *His Majesty*, but to Blotto the deprivation had felt like a lifetime. He swallowed down the first mouthful of his St Louis Steamhammer and waited for the firecrackers to detonate inside his cranium.

As the pyrotechnic display began, continuing life seemed once more a possibility. Even the prospect of marriage to Mary Chapstick was momentarily less daunting.

Apparently divining the direction of his thoughts, Spagsy Chiaparelli said, 'You're marrying the Chapstick broad.'

'That is the plan, yes. We're twiddling up the old reef-knot at some church I've yet to have the pleasure of meeting, and then the reception's going to be held in the Chainey Hotel . . . which I gather you own . . .?'

'I own it, yeah. I own most of Chicago.'

'Well, that's a rum baba. Because Luther P. Chapstick III says he owns most of it too.'

Spagsy Chiaparelli let out what had to be assumed to be a chuckle, though it caused no change of expression on his granite features. 'Let's say Chapstick and I have an understanding. Between us we cover the waterfront.'

'Just the waterfront?'

'When I say waterfront what I mean is the entire city.'

'Ah. Hoopee-doopee for you,' said Blotto. 'The city you're talking about is Chicago?'

'What other city were you thinking of?'

'I don't know. I just wondered if you might happen to own New York as well.'

That shook Spagsy Chiaparelli. He focused his cold grey eyes on the blond-haired young man in front of him. Could this dumb cluck of an Englishman actually know of his hidden plans, the secret deal he'd been working on with the *capo dei capi* of the New York mafia, Harry 'Three Bananas' Pennoni? Could he know about the millions of dollars' worth of gold bullion stolen from the US government with which he'd agreed to pay Pennoni for a slice of the Big Apple action? Was this duke not as stupid as he appeared to be? Was his 'silly ass' demeanour in fact a cunning front for an extremely devious undercover operator—possibly even one sent from New York by Pennoni to check

110

the Chicago set-up?

Spagsy knew he had to proceed with caution. 'Tell me, Duke,' he said, 'are you a member of *Cosa Nostra*?'

'No,' Blotto replied. 'I'm Church of England.'

Spagsy Chiaparelli's anxieties about the newcomer having a cunning front receded.

The band came to the end of another song. There was silence. They were clearly about to take a break but waiting for permission. Then Spagsy started clapping and the rest of the room followed his lead. He looked piercingly at the Englishman. 'You like music?'

Blotto looked across at the singer. 'I do when it's sung by a breathsapper like that.'

'You reckon the chanteuse is a good-looking broad?'

'I'll say! She's absolutely the nun's nightie.'

'You taken a fancy to her, have you?'

Blotto was about to say that he thought she was a real bellbuzzer with three veg and gravy, when he became aware of a change in the quality of the silence around the table. Once again an uncharacteristic insight warned him that expressing too much interest in the singer might not be a tactful move, so far as Spagsy Chiaparelli was concerned. So he revised his response and just said, 'She sings very well.'

The boss nodded, as if accepting the compliment personally, then looked up as the subject of their discussion sauntered across the room towards them. The closer she got, the better she looked to Blotto, and it was sad that he didn't yet know the word 'sexy', because there really was no other way to describe her. What made the singer's approach even more exciting was the fact that she seemed to be heading straight for him.

But just as Blotto was about to become engulfed in her aura of expensive perfume, she found her real destination, the seat next to his, where she dressed herself artfully over Spagsy Chiaparelli. 'Hi, babe,' said the Boss in a manner that was very definitely proprietorial.

'Hi,' she responded, her voice still as smoky as when she was singing. Then she turned her hazel eyes on Blotto and asked, 'Who's the dreamboat?'

Blotto wasn't quite sure what a dreamboat was, but her look implied it was not something totally unattractive.

'This is the Duke of Leicester,' replied Spagsy, further mangling his name and title.

'Wow!' said the chanteuse. 'A genuine English aristocrat?'

Blotto made no response but for a sheepish grin.

'Lady asked if you were a genuine English aristocrat,' Spagsy Chiaparelli prompted.

'Oh yes. The genuine article. Family goes nearly all the way back to the Norman Conquest. Nothing leadpenny about me.'

'Gee.' The singer favoured him with a sultry smile. 'I've never met a genuine English aristocrat before.' She stretched a white hand out towards him. 'Pleased to meetcha. I'm Choxy Mulligan.'

Blotto wasn't sure whether the hand was being proffered to be kissed or shaken. Seeing the ominously total lack of expression in Spagsy Chiaparelli's face, he shook it. 'Very nice to meet you too, Miss Mulligan.'

'Choxy,' she insisted. 'Everybody calls me Choxy.'

A raucous laugh came from one of the other men

at the table who'd also overindulged alcoholically. 'Just like everyone calls your boyfriend Spagsy!'

After he too had been shot by Chiaparelli—quite legally, of course, he was another multiple murderer—and his body disposed of (the police helping once again), Choxy Mulligan said she'd like a bourbon on the rocks, which was instantly supplied to her.

One hand held the drink as she sipped it, while the other twisted a tendril of red hair as she looked across at Blotto from under thick eyelashes. 'You're a real dish,' she said.

'Am I?' asked Blotto, again not familiar with the expression, but reckoning a dish was probably something on roughly the same lines as a dreamboat. And therefore not unflattering.

Spagsy Chiaparelli clearly didn't like the direction the conversation was taking. 'Cut that out, Choxy!' he snapped. 'Unless you're looking to get yourself beat up again. I know you got the morals of an alley cat, but this one's already spoken for.'

'Oh?'

'The chimp's gonna marry old Chapstick's girl.'

Choxy Mulligan pouted. 'What a waste.'

'Hey, come on, get that drink down your throat. You're paid to sing here, Choxy, not to cosy up to the clientele.'

She pouted again, but she knew not to stretch her patron's patience too far. Slurping back her bourbon, Choxy Mulligan said, 'Sure, we'll get on with the next set,' and slinked deliciously back towards the bandstand. As she passed Blotto, her body shielding what she was doing from Spagsy, he could have sworn she slipped something into his top pocket. But no, thought Blotto, that's so unlikely as to be completely ridiculous. He must have imagined it.

At another table, she trailed a hand lasciviously along one man's shoulder. He reached up to touch it. Spagsy Chiaparelli shot him.

Blotto smiled. 'Don't tell me—multiple murderer?'

'That's it exactly.'

'How many this time?'

Spagsy looked around the table. 'Thirty-two,' his acolytes agreed.

As Choxy Mulligan started to sing again, some of the men (helped of course by the police) busied themselves with removing the latest corpse. Blotto sat back in a kind of bliss, sipping his drink and letting the voice of the chanteuse wash over him like liquid chocolate.

My man don't love me,
'Cept when he wants me.
He don't sweet-talk me,
He only taunts me.
My man don't call me,
But still he haunts me.
With him I'm always playing
Second fiddle to the booze,
And that's why I'm always singing
Those man-thirsty blues.

Blotto was struck that there did seem to be quite a recurrence of subject matter in Choxy Mulligan's songs.

At the end of the evening, warmed by a good few more St Louis Steamhammers, he staggered out to find a cab. This took a surprisingly long time, the only ones he saw for a while being occupied by groups of men who kept shooting at groups of men in other cabs.

But while he waited and thought about his evening, mellowed by the Steamhammers, Blotto came to realize what a frightfully decent chap Spagsy Chiaparelli actually was. Definitely a force for good. Not in the conventional way, of course. Rather more like Robin Hood, an outlaw devoted to the cause of justice. Well, fair biddles to him. He'd probably been tracking all those multiple murderers for years and set up that particular evening to entrap them. That would explain why all the police had been present. And though that wasn't exactly the way that kind of thing would be done in England, the criminals had undoubtedly deserved to suffer the death penalty. Maybe, Blotto thought in his increasingly benign mood, our way isn't necessarily always the best way. Perhaps the British system of justice has something to learn from the more immediate methods employed by our American cousins.

Blearily, as the cab he'd finally found drove him out of the city towards Chapstick Towers, Blotto remembered that strange sensation he'd had when Choxy Mulligan had passed him on the way back to the bandstand. Surely he'd been mistaken . . .? She hadn't really put anything in his top pocket, had she?

But he reached into it, just to be sure, and his hand closed round a piece of paper.

From the light of the occasional streetlamps he was able to read what was on it. A sequence of numbers. A kind of code perhaps. Definitely not the kind of thing he could work out. Something for

Twinks, thought Blotto as he sank deeply into a St Louis Steamhammered sleep.

15

Twinks Has a Plan

Mercifully, by the time Blotto got back to Chapstick Towers Mary had returned from her evening with the bridesmaids and retired for the night. Of her father there was no sign. Which meant Blotto could go straight to his sister's bedroom. Ever resourceful, Twinks had packed in her reticule a travel kettle, saucepan and small gas ring on which she was soon preparing cocoa. It was almost like the sessions the siblings had shared in her boudoir at Tawcester Towers . . . except of course that they were in alien territory a long way from home. And they still had a major marriage-sized problem to solve.

But Twinks was in the most gleeful state that her brother had seen her since their arrival in the United States. She was bubbling with excitement, eager to share with Blotto the discoveries she had made in Luther P. Chapstick III's study.

'He's certainly up to something very murdey.'

'Oh,' said Blotto, whose brain was still rather scrambled by the St Louis Steamhammers.

'To do with the Katzenjammers.'

'Oh,' he said again, but her words had started to clear the fumes of alcohol. He remembered that Twinks had been out to discover some link between Chapstick and his arch-rival. And it sounded like she'd found it. Maybe they were already on the way to getting Mary Chapstick's engagement to Sophocles Katzenjammer reconstituted . . .?

'I found plans in Luther P. Chapstick III's desk for an act of serious sabotage against the Katzenjammers.'

'Did you, by Denzil?'

'I took copies of them with the miniature camera I always carry in my reticule,' she announced, removing a sheaf of papers from the said receptacle.

Blotto looked at the dense pages of tightly written text. They blurred and oscillated beneath his scrutiny. 'Just hit me with the headlines, could you, Twinks?'

'Righty-ho. You'll find this stuff's really grandissimo, Blotters me old sock suspender. What Chapstick is planning to do is to infiltrate some of his boddos into the Katzenjammers' factory and get them to put poison in the entire stock of Katzenjammer Beef Extract. Getting great jeroboamsful of people really sick, maybe a few even dying . . . well, that's going to make the Katzenjammer Stilton pretty iffy, isn't it? No company's ever going to recover from that kind of bad publicity.'

'Maybe not, Twinks me old warming-pan. But I don't quite see how this fits my pigeon-hole.'

'It'll fit it, Blotto me old banana flambé, because I am going to reveal Chapstick's evil plan to the Katzenjammers. I've already had copies of these papers sent to them by a secret courier. There's going to be one hell of a stinkbomb going off when they find out what old Luther's up to.'

'Maybe. But I still don't see quite how that's going to help tug me out of the treacle tin.'

'It will help you by proving that Luther P. Chapstick III is a thumping great crook! And surely, once it's known that he's capable of that kind of . . .'

Her words trickled away. Even as she spoke them, she realized the glaring hole in her logic. She had been so carried away by the thrill of her quest in Chapstick's study that she had forgotten one of the basic rules of life in the Lyminster family.

It was a rare moment for Blotto. Not often did his sister make that kind of error (any kind of error, actually). At other times he might have rubbed her nose in it, even resorting to the nursery put-down: 'So Snubbins to you!' But on this occasion, perhaps from the benignity all those St Louis Steamhammers had produced in him, or his natural good nature, he didn't glory in the moment of triumph. He just confirmed the known truth. 'It wouldn't make a blind bezonger's bit of difference with the mater, would it?'

'No,' Twinks admitted wretchedly.

'She's not going to worry that the man with whose daughter I'm about to have the reef-knot twiddled turns out to be a criminal, is she?'

Another wretched 'Oh.'

'I mean, that kind of thing's never mattered too much with people of our sort, has it? You only have to think how most members of the British aristocracy got their titles in the first place, don't you?'

It was self-evidently true. The historical route into the upper echelons of British society had usually involved such services as beating up the monarch's enemies, providing royal mistresses or stealing from the poor to subsidize the lavish royal lifestyle. Someone like the Dowager Duchess of Tawcester, brought up with those kind of values, would not regard a minor misdemeanour like potentially poisoning an entire population (particularly when that population consisted only of Americans) as any bar to her son's marriage.

'So we're back in the same gluepot, aren't we?' said Blotto mournfully.

'There's got to be a way out!' his sister asserted. The colour passion brought to her cheeks made her more beautiful than ever. 'We're Lyminsters! When the going gets a bit dicky, we don't just fold up like theatre programmes!' Her perfect forehead furrowed with the effort of thought. 'Maybe there still is something in the Katzenjammer connection . . .? Knowing about Chapstick's evil plans might put them on our side. Then perhaps this Sophocles Katzenjammer booby will step in as understudy for your part in the Mary Chapstick wedding circus . . .?'

'Perhaps.' Blotto didn't sound optimistic. 'But from what Mary's said of her father's attitude to the Katzenjammers, he'd just never let it happen.'

'No.' Frustration welled up in Twinks. It wasn't only that she was accustomed to getting her own way, it was also that she regarded the current situation as a reflection of her personal inadequacy. Her much-vaunted brainbox wasn't living up to its vaunts. 'Anyway,' she said listlessly, 'how was your evening?'

So Blotto gave her a Steamhammer-by-Steamhammer account of events at the Chainey Hotel and in the secret speakeasy behind it. He finished on a high note. 'The really beezer thing about it, though, is that I have proved it is possible to get a drink in this bliss-bereft country. I think from now on I'm going to stay permanently wobbulated. It's the only way I'm going to get through this wocky wedding.'

'And, Blotters, how was it the singer described you?'

He blushed to the roots of his corn-gold hair. 'A "dreamboat", I think . . . and a "dish" . . .' Twinks looked thoughtful. 'What are you having a cogitette about then, eh?'

'Just wondering . . . if maybe this singer . . .'

'Choxy Mulligan.'

'Exactly. If she might be our way out of the gluepot . . .'

'How?'

'Well, if she really has chosen you off the menu . . .'

'Oh, I wouldn't go that far,' said Blotto, embarrassed again.

'Then maybe if you were to giddy-up her interest, Mary Chapstick might get to hear about it and . . . who knows what might happen? Did this Choxy do anything else, except look at you like a pike at a troutling?'

'Well, she did actually shove a piece of paper in my pocket . . .'

'Show me.'

As ever, Blotto followed his sister's instructions. 'I think it must be some kind of code.'

'No, it isn't,' said Twinks.

'Then what is it?'

'It's a telephone number. Choxy Mulligan has given you her telephone number!'

Blotto looked puzzled. 'Why on earth would she do that?'

'Because . . .' Twinks clapped her hands together with glee. 'Oh, this is larksissimo! This is playing right into our hands. Blotto, our troubles are really at an end!'

'How?'

'Because Choxy Mulligan has given you her phone number!'

'Yes, but what should I do with it?'

'What should you do with it? You should ring her, Blotto me old fruitbasket!'

16

Sticking to the Script

While Tawcester Towers only boasted a single telephone in its draughty hall, Chapstick Towers seemed to have one in virtually every room. And though both Blotto and Twinks would in normal circumstances have disapproved of such ostentation, the following morning they were very glad of it. Luther P. Chapstick III had not yet returned from the Chainey Hotel and his daughter had mercifully gone out on the one mission on which her fiancé couldn't accompany her—a fitting for her wedding dress. So the siblings had a wide choice of telephonic apparatus from which to make the pivotal call. They decided to do it from the one in Blotto's bedroom.

Having woken with his head still pounding from the effect of the St Louis Steamhammers, Blotto had also woken with a guilty conscience. He remembered Mary Chapstick's words about the pain for a woman of being stood up, and yet that would be the effect of putting their current plan into action. It took all of his sister's powers of persuasion to get him back on the right track.

'Listen, Blotters me old riding crop,' she said. 'Desperate circumstances call for desperate measures. I know when it comes to being honourable, you're a Grade A foundation stone, but we've never been in a gluier gluepot than the present one. You don't love Mary, do you?'

'Well, she's a pleasant enough old pineapple, not to mention a bit of a breathsapper, and I'm sure she could make some lucky boddo feel like he'd won the raffle. But I'm not that boddo. So no, I don't love her.'

'But she loves you . . .'

He winced. 'Does she?'

'No way round it. She's got all the symptoms. That kind of permanent soupiness of expression can only mean one thing.'

'Oh, broken biscuits.'

'But the thing is, Blotters, marriage can only work if there's equal love on both sides. That's been a well-known fact since Adam popped the question to Eve. If you twiddle the reef-knot with Mary Chapstick, you'll be condemning her to a life of unhappiness.'

'Sorry, not on the same page?'

'Women,' pronounced Twinks with the authority of her gender, 'not only want to love, they want to inspire love. Mary will pretty soon realize that you don't love her, and she'll spend the rest of her married life trying to make you do so. And what chance does she have of doing that?'

'About as much chance as I have of playing

croquet with Henry VIII.'

'Exactly. So if you marry the poor old thimble, you'll be condemning her to a lifetime of misery and frustration.'

'Toad-in-the-hole!' said Blotto. 'Now you put it like that . . .'

Twinks pressed home her advantage. 'Marrying her would be an act of great cruelty. The greatest kindness you can do to Mary Chapstick is to stand her up. It's the only honourable course.'

Still Blotto looked undecided. While recognizing the power of his sister's argument, he couldn't forget the promise he had given to the girl. More than that, he couldn't forget the Dowager Duchess's likely reaction to his crying off from the wedding. He felt himself to be on the horns of one of those things beginning with a 'd' whose name he could never remember.

'Besides,' said Twinks silkily, 'how do you feel about never playing cricket again and spending the rest of your life watching rounders?'

Needless to say, that clinched it. Any moral qualms Blotto may have been feeling were instantly swallowed. 'You're right, Twinks me old tin tray! As ever. So . . . what's the next step on the staircase?'

'You have to ring the number Choxy Mulligan gave you, and tell her that the attraction between you is mutual. You have to come on really strong.'

'Mm.' He looked troubled. 'I think I may be a bit of an empty revolver when it's a matter of coming on strong.'

'Well, you must try. Remember what's at stake, Blotto. Rounders . . .' she repeated, knowing exactly how to screw her brother's courage to the sticking place.

'Good ticket,' said Blotto. 'I'll come on strong to Choxy Mulligan.'

While pleased that he was taking the task seriously, Twinks was still a little worried as to whether his idea of 'coming on strong' coincided with her own. 'Blotto, when you get through to her on the phone, what will you actually say?'

'Ooh, that's a bit of a stumper, sis.' He tapped his chin thoughtfully. 'Erm . . . probably "hello" . . .?' he hazarded.

Twinks could find no objection to that. 'And then what?'

'Well, I'd probably say how I got her phone number.'

'She knows that.'

'So she does. So I might say that at first I thought what she'd given me was a code, but then my sister told me it was a phone number and—'

'Keep me out of it!'

'Why, Twinks? I want you involved in everything in my life.'

'Men in the throes of unassuageable passion do not as a rule consult their sisters about it.'

'Oh. And is that what I'm in the throes of? "Unassuageable passion"?'

'I think, if our little planette is going to work, then you must appear to be.'

'Good ticket.' There was a long silence. 'How?'

Now Twinks was uniquely qualified to answer this question. Fatally attractive as she was, she had spent much of her young life witnessing many amorous swains in the paroxysms of unassuageable passion. So she knew whereof she spoke when she replied to her brother, 'Men change when they are in love. Even the most hard-boiled

124

suddenly become runny. They are hypersensitive to the slightest of slights from the object of their adoration. Their eyes tend to go poppy and they take on the expression of constipated bullfrogs. They burble a lot and are unable to think of anything but their beloved.'

After a silence, Blotto cautiously admitted that he could probably do the burbling bit. 'But I'm not so sure about the rest of it.'

'You have to be extremely ardent as you press your suit.'

'But I don't press my own suits. Tweedling does that kind of guff for me.'

'No, I meant . . .' But Twinks didn't bother to pursue the explanation. 'Listen, Blotto, haven't you ever felt the stirrings of passion?'

'Don't think so. Not for a woman, anyway.'

'Well imagine we were talking about the Lagonda . . .'

'Aah.' An expression of contentment settled on Blotto's impossibly handsome features.

'. . . or Mephistopheles . . .'

'Mmm.' The contentment took on a tone of greater passion.

'. . . or your cricket bat . . .'

'Now you're talking!' His manly features glowed as he waxed lyrical. 'That bat's got me out of more gluepots than you've had amorous swains, Twinks me old biscuit barrel. It was made from the finest willow and, even though it's now scarred with the memories of boundaries in many matches, the old breathsapper's still a thing of great beauty. When I anoint its surface with linseed oil, I feel as if I'm part of some ancient mystery, almost a religious rite. It has more power and dignity even than

Mephistopheles. That cricket bat is more precious to me than life itself!'

'Grandissimo, Blotters! Now all you've got to do is translate some of that passion into your forthcoming conversation with Choxy Mulligan.'

'Hoopee-doopee!'

'Do you think you can do it?'

'Yes, by Denzil!'

'So what's the first thing you'll say to her when you get through?'

'"Hello."'

'Yes, I think we've established that. What next?'

'Erm. "You know, Choxy, I feel the same way about you as I do my cricket bat."'

'Ye-es. I'm not absolutely convinced that this is going to work, Blotto me old kipper zipper. Do you think it might help if I were to write something?'

'What, more of your translation of Montyflipmadoodle?'

'No. A kind of script for you.'

'Script?'

'Yes, I write down a list of things for you to say to Choxy Mulligan. Things that will convince her that you are suffering from unassuageable passion for her.'

'Ah, I read your semaphore, yes. Beezer idea, Twinks!'

It was a matter of moments for his sister's nimble brain to provide a narrative for his forthcoming conversation. She passed the sheet of paper across and Blotto looked at it with the same reverence he so often evinced for her achievements. 'Toad-in-the-hole, Twinks! You really are the lark's larynx. Whatever stuff it is inside your brainbox, there's not a lot of it about. These lines'll absolutely fit the

126

pigeon-hole so far as Choxy Mulligan is concerned. I'm sure the woman hasn't been born who could resist this lot. How do you do it?'

'Oh, it's as easy as raspberries once you get going,' said his sister modestly.

Blotto scanned the sheet. 'So, what, do I say these lines to her in this order?'

'No, no. Depends on what she says. Just sprinkle them into the conversation.'

'Sprinkle?'

'Yes, sprinkle.'

'Hoopee-doopee!'

Twinks casually picked up her reticule. 'I must go downstairs.'

'What? Why? You're not going to leave me to do this on my solo, are you?'

'I'm just going to check that the coast is clear. If Mr Chapstick or Mary came back and found you making the phone call you're about to make . . . well . . .'

Blotto nodded ruefully. 'Do you think I should ring her straight away?' he asked, his feet chilling a little.

'You've got to do it now, Blotto. Come on strong to her, don't get off the telephone until you have fixed a time to meet her. It's our only way out of this particular treacle tin.'

'Yes, but . . .'

She fixed her brother with the Dowager Duchess's Gorgon stare and he nodded unhappy compliance.

Suddenly Twinks was gone. Blotto looked again at the list she had given him, then at the piece of paper Choxy Mulligan had thrust into his pocket. No way round it. Twinks was right. What had to be done had to be done.

He couldn't help once again admiring his sister's skill as he looked through the lines she had written.

I couldn't sleep last night for thinking of you.

There's no time in my life for thoughts that have nothing to do with you.

I can't stand the thought of being without you.

My idea of heaven would be being alone with you.

If you refused to be my lover, my life would be in ruins.

If you were in my arms, I'd have everything I've ever wanted.

No one in the world is more beautiful than you are.

Every woman I've ever met is really ugly compared to you.

I'll be in an agony of disappointment until we actually meet.

You'll be my favourite fantasy for the rest of my life.

He put the sheet on his lap and reached for the telephone. He removed the speaker and juggled its rest until the operator answered. He gave the number, there were a few whirrings and clicks, then the unmistakably smoky voice of Choxy Mulligan said, 'Hello.'

'Hello.' Having delivered his only personal contribution to the script, he looked down the list for the next suitable rejoinder.

But before he had time to choose one, Choxy asked, 'Who is this?'

'My name's Blotto. Well, I wasn't introduced to you as that. In fact, they got my name wrong. Boddo said I was the Duke of Leicester, whereas in fact—'

'Oh, hi,' the chanteuse purred. 'You're the bit of beefcake from last night.'

Blotto mentally added 'beefcake' to 'dreamboat' and 'dish' on the list of words he didn't know but reckoned were complimentary.

'So, I'm glad you rang,' Choxy Mulligan husked. 'And what do you have to say to me?'

'Erm ...' Blotto looked down at the list on his knees, but a nervous hand flicked it on to the floor. Desperate, trying to remember what was on the sheet and mindful that Twinks said men in love could be recognized by their burbling, he burbled out, speeding up as his nerves took hold, 'I couldn't sleep last night for thoughts that have nothing to do with you. There's no time in my life for thinking of you. I can't stand the thought of being alone with you. My idea of heaven would be being without you. If you were in my arms, my life would be in ruins. If you refused to be my lover, I'd have everything I've ever wanted. Every woman I've ever met is more beautiful than you are. No one in the world is really ugly compared to you. You'll be my favourite fantasy until we actually meet. I'll be in an agony of disappointment for the rest of my life.'

Blotto drew breath. 'What the hell,' asked Choxy Mulligan, 'was all that about?'

'Erm ...'

'Are you saying you'd like us to meet?'

'Erm ... well ... yes.'

'OK. Come to my place six o'clock this evening. Cocktail hour. We'll start with a cocktail and then ...' she breathed heavily into the receiver '... see where we go from there.' She gave him the address.

Blotto put the telephone down with some relief. And satisfaction. He thought he'd managed the conversation rather well.

17

Blotto and the Moll

As he guided the Lagonda from Chapstick Towers into Chicago that evening, Blotto reflected once again on the perverseness of the Americans. Driving on the left-hand side of the road was so obvious, so natural. There was a bit of a pointer, for those who could see it, in the way cars were designed, for the love of strawberries! The steering wheel of the Lagonda was on the right, so that the driver could see the oncoming traffic. It wasn't a very difficult concept, but the Americans just didn't seem to be able to understand the simplest things. Again, like that business of saying 'gotten' when they meant 'got'.

But he was feeling the first un-St Louis Steamhammered peace he'd had since he arrived in the United States. Partly, being at the wheel of the Lagonda always gave him a sense of contentment. And that was augmented by the knowledge that he'd got his cricket bat safely stowed in a valise in the back. He didn't really know why he had brought it, but he felt he needed some talisman, some good luck charm to see him through his encounter with Choxy Mulligan.

He also felt good because Twinks had finally devised a plan to get him out of his unwelcome engagement. For too long her Grade A brainbox hadn't been living up to its reputation, but now she had finally come up with the silverware. When Blotto's name was publicly linked to that of the chanteuse Choxy Mulligan, Luther P. Chapstick III would have no alternative but to call off the wedding.

And he no longer felt guilty about what they were proposing to do. What Twinks had said about the misery of unrequited love inside a marriage had really struck home with him. And seeing the soupy looks Mary Chapstick had cast at him over lunch had only strengthened his resolve. The way she kept on about her wedding dress (coyly revealing no details of what it actually looked like) had made him feel positively sorry for the poor little thimble. She deserved better than the life sentence of a loveless marriage.

He was still feeling a bit nervous about the evening ahead, but determined to go through with it. All he had to do was to meet Choxy Mulligan in compromising circumstances and let the rumours flow that they were having some kind of beyond-the-barbed-wire ding-dong. The news would soon enough get to Luther P. Chapstick III and he would immediately forbid his daughter's alliance with such a four-faced stencher. There'd be the odd awkward scene, no doubt, but very soon Blotto, Twinks and the precious Lagonda would be on the first available liner back to Blighty. Mary Chapstick would no doubt be hurt in the short term, but later in life, sharing requited love with the right man, she would realize what a narrow shave she had had, and be grateful to Blotto for doing the gentlemanly thing by doing an ungentlemanly thing.

And as for fears about news of his churlish behaviour reaching Tawcester Towers ... well, he wasn't worried on that score. Blotto's sort of people had no interest in events that took place in the United States (or indeed in anywhere else that wasn't England). True, the Dowager Duchess would be put a little out of joint when he returned without the Chapstick millions, but she'd have to find another way to sort out the Tawcester Towers plumbing. All Blotto'd need to do would be airily to tell her that for no accountable reason Luther P. Chapstick III had suddenly turned against him. (Even as he had that thought he recognized that his manner might not be quite so airy when actually confronting his mother in the Blue Morning Room, but he'd worry about that later.)

He parked the Lagonda easily opposite the address that Choxy Mulligan had given him. As he left it, unlocked (he always left it unlocked in England), he noticed a couple of men loitering outside the entrance to the unnecessarily tall apartment block. They both carried violin cases and did look astonishingly like two of the men who'd been at Spagsy Chiaparelli's table the night before. But Blotto decided that'd be too much of a coincidence. Clearly there was a 'Chicago type'. Just as Welshmen were short, dark and wiry, so men in this part of Illinois all had beetling brows, granite features, thick-set bodies, double-breasted pinstriped suits and violin cases.

The man behind the desk in the apartment block's lobby also looked familiar, but again Blotto dismissed the possibility that he'd seen him the previous evening. Another of the 'Chicago type', sitting there with his violin case in front of him.

He asked for Choxy Mulligan. The heavy checked with the intercom and established that she was expecting him, then directed the visitor to the elevator and the eighteenth floor. Once again

132

Blotto mentally tutted about the gratuitous height of American buildings. It was just another form of showing off, really.

Strange look the man on the desk gave him as he walked to the elevator. Mixture of disbelief, admiration and amusement. Blotto couldn't think why. Nor could he think why the man was already whispering into the telephone by the time he'd entered the elevator.

On the eighteenth floor he walked along to the relevant apartment, lifted the knocker and gave two sharp raps. There was a moment's pause and then the door opened.

He was immediately aware of cool jazz playing softly from a gramophone, an overpowering musky perfume and in the background another smell, almost like burning grass cuttings.

He was also immediately aware of Choxy Mulligan. She had given up the black of the night before for bright green, the skirt stopping impishly above her white-stockinged knees. Green strapped shoes and coils of white pearls dangling from her neck to below her waist. The cap of red hair and the generous slash of red lipstick were as striking as they had been on first encounter. She really was a splendid piece of womanflesh.

'Come in,' she susurrated.

Blotto did as he was bidden and found himself in a candlelit Aladdin's Cave of dropping draperies and beaded curtains. Choxy Mulligan shut the door behind him and leant against it, taking in the full sight of him with rather embarrassing relish.

'Gee!' she murmured. 'You really are some hunk, aintcher, Duke?'

'I'm not actually a duke.'

133

'Who cares when you look like you do? Whadda people call you?'

'Blotto.'

'Blotto?' She looked perplexed for a moment, then shrugged and said, 'Blotto it is then. Can I get you a drink?'

'Please.'

'I've just prepared a shaker of martini. Dry as a temperance Christmas. Over there on the tray. Pour them for us. I take an olive.'

Pouring the drinks into the shallow cone-shaped glasses did not prove too much of a challenge. When Blotto turned back, he found Choxy had draped herself over a sofa in a manner that revealed an eye-boggling amount of white-stockinged thigh (and even a hint of suspender at the top). She patted the space at her side. 'Join me.'

He did as instructed. (Having grown up with the Dowager Duchess in the house, he never argued with what a woman told him to do.) Close to, he felt enveloped in the heady aura of her musky perfume.

'So, Blotto, here we are.'

'Here we are indeed. Hoopee-doopee.'

There was a silence. Blotto began to wish he'd brought Twinks's list of suitable things to say to Choxy Mulligan. Except, of course, she might have noticed if he started reading.

On the principle that you can never have too many 'Hoopee-doopees', he once again said, 'Hoopee-doopee.'

'You say you're not a duke, Blotto . . .'

'No.'

'Then what are you?'

'I'm the younger son of a duke.'

'Oh. Is that bad?'

'Well, it's not as good as being a duke . . . that is if you like being a duke.'

'And would you like being a duke?'

Blotto thought about his brother Loofah spending his entire life devoted to the cause of impregnating his wife Sloggo with something other than a girl, and said that he wouldn't.

'So what do you do?' asked Choxy Mulligan.

Blotto was perplexed by the question but still replied, 'People of my sort don't *do* anything.'

He took a sip from his martini. Though without the immediate brain-shredding impact of a St Louis Steamhammer, it was still very good.

'One thing's puzzled me since I've been here, Choxy,' he said. 'I keep hearing from boddos that the manufacture and sale of alcohol is forbidden, but people still seem to be able to get drinks. How does that work?'

'It's a matter of having the right friends.'

'Is it, by Wilberforce?'

'And I've got a very good friend.' She chuckled throatily. 'A rather rough kinda fairy godfather called Spagsy Chiaparelli.'

'And he supplies you with the booze?'

'He supplies Chicago with the booze.'

'That's very public-spirited of him. Bringing alcohol to the deprived. Rather like those St Flipmadoodle dogs who bring brandy to stranded travellers in the Alps.'

'I don't know what you're talking about, Blotto, but I do love listening to your voice.'

'Oh, good ticket. I must say I was very impressed last night by Mr Chiaparelli's rather unusual approach to justice. He's a very dedicated public servant, isn't he?'

'Oh, you can say that again.' She turned the full beam of her smoky blue eyes on him. 'You're very brave, Blotto. I like that in a man.'

'Oh, it's nothing, really. Anyway, why do you say I'm brave?'

'You came to see me.'

'It wasn't too hard a rusk to chew. The doorman turned out to be a very helpful boddo.'

Choxy Mulligan's white hands leapt up to cover her appalled face. 'You let the doorman see you?'

'Why shouldn't I?'

'That doorman is Boggy "Two Noses" Taormina.' Admiration replaced horror in her face. 'Wow, you're quite a man, aren't you, Blotto? Just stepping right out and challenging him like that.'

'Challenging who? The doorman?'

'Spagsy. Spagsy Chiaparelli.'

'What's he got to do with anything? I mean, apart from his good works in supplying booze and justice?'

'Surely you realize, Blotto, that I'm Spagsy's girl? I'm his very close friend. His moll. His *goomar*.'

'Ah,' he said, trying to work this out. Perhaps he should have pieced it together from the way she had draped herself over Chiaparelli the previous evening. 'But if you're already spoken for, why did you give me your telephone number?'

'To see what kind of a man you are. And now I've seen. And I like what I see. Kiss me,' she commanded.

Blotto ventured further into the heady miasma of her perfume and planted a kiss on her powdered cheek. The sensation was not unpleasant.

As he drew back, Choxy Mulligan snarled, 'Call that a kiss?'

'Well, that's what it's called in England,' he replied.

'But what about lips?'

'I did actually use my lips,' said Blotto, slightly put out that she hadn't noticed.

'What about *my* lips?'

'Tickey-tockey.' Blotto offered his cheek to be kissed.

'Are you just playing dumb or are you the real McCoy?'

'My name's Blotto,' he said. 'I thought you knew that.'

'Forget it.' She snuggled up close, almost asphyxiating him with her musky perfume, and running her fingers up and down his thigh. 'I like men who're dangerous.'

'Oh, I wouldn't say I'm dangerous. I'm rather a whale on the concept of honour, actually. You'll be quite safe with me.'

'Who wants to be safe?' Choxy Mulligan purred, increasing the pressure of her thigh-stroking.

Blotto had heard the expression 'getting hot under the collar', but he wasn't sure that he'd ever felt it. But he was feeling it now. He eased a finger round the inside of the relevant article of clothing and abruptly stood up, moving towards the window.

'Hey, what's up, dreamboat?' asked Choxy.

Blotto improvised desperately. 'Um, just wanted to check the old Lag's all tickey-tockey.'

Through the beaded curtains he looked down to the street and saw that the Lagonda was far from tickey-tockey. Where he had parked it there was now just a space.

A moment behind this discovery came the realization that his precious cricket bat was in the car. Two of his most prized possessions had disappeared in one fell swoop.

In the heat of emotion he managed to blurt out, 'My car's gone!'

'Wodja say?' asked Choxy.

'My car. My Lagonda. I parked it right opposite and it's not there any more.'

'Oh, that kinda thing happens a lot round here. The doorman will have taken it.'

'What, to park it somewhere safe?'

Choxy Mulligan was about to say where the car would really be taken, but she didn't want to provide any further distractions to Blotto, so she just let out a reassuring 'Yeah.' Then she once again patted the sofa beside her. 'Come back here.'

Blotto moved across and perched rather gingerly on the edge of the upholstery.

'Tell me, Blotto,' Choxy asked huskily, 'how do you come to be so brave?'

'I don't really know, but one of my beaks at Eton used to pongle on about "cowards dying many times before their deaths", some quotation from ... I don't know, the Bible possibly ...? Anyway, the gist of what this beak said was that people only got afraid because they imagined murdey things happening. And since I had no imagination, I was never going to be afraid of anything.'

This was quite a long speech for Blotto, and also contained a greater depth of self-analysis than he usually allowed himself. He felt quite exhausted after it.

'Well, bravery in a man really gets me excited,' murmured Choxy, her hand back in thigh-stroking mode. 'The way you've just come to see me, openly, without any security measures.'

'What would I want with security measures?'

'Look, pretty soon all of Chicago's going to know you and me've got a thing going on.'

'Hoopee-doopee! That's the aim of the exercise.'

'Howdja mean?'

'I want all Chicago to know about us! I want it shouted from the rooftops regularly on the hour. "Blotto is having a thing with Choxy Mulligan!" The more people know about it, the better.'

'Even Spagsy?'

'Yes, of course Spagsy. Because Spagsy has an understanding with Luther P. Chapstick III, so the old meat-packing magnate will very quickly hear about what's supposed to be going on.'

'And why are you so cheerful about that happening?'

'Well, old Chapstick's not going to be so keen on his daughter twiddling the reef-knot with some boddo who's consorting with a woman of dubious morals.'

'Are you suggesting my morals are dubious?'

'Yes.'

'Good.' She hugged herself with satisfaction. 'That's the way I've always wanted them to be.' The arm that wasn't engaged in stroking his thigh coiled itself around Blotto's manly shoulders. 'Anyway, I think we should get on with the "consorting", don't you?'

'Oh, we don't actually have to do anything.'

'What?'

'I'm not the kind of lump of toadspawn who'd take advantage of a lady.'

'Even when that lady wanted you to take advantage of her?'

'Erm ... Um ...' He didn't quite know how

139

to answer that question. 'Look, the thing is ... I know in one way it's not very honourable and all that, but if Mary Chapstick marries me she will be condemned to a life of suffering, because her love can never be reciprocated. And my sister and I were thinking of ways to get out of that particular gluepot, when I remembered the piece of paper you put in my pocket. Suddenly—there was the solution. I'm seen to be consorting with a woman of dubious morals—something on which, as you say, you pride yourself—old Chapstick hears about it—end of engagement! All tickey-tockey wouldn't you say?'

This speech had an effect on Choxy Mulligan that Blotto wouldn't have predicted (but then he wasn't much good at predicting anything where women were concerned). Abruptly she removed both hands from his body and when she spoke it was in a snarl rather than a purr.

'You two-faced hornswoggler!' she cried.

'Sorry?' said Blotto.

'Are you telling me you don't find me attractive?'

'Toad-in-the-hole, no. I think you're a real breathsapper with veg and all the trimmings.'

'But you don't want to "consort" with me?'

'Not really, if it's all the same to you.'

'Hell, look, I gave you my number because you're the kind of hunk of beefcake who gets my juices flowing. When you called and said you wanted to see me, I thought it was because the attraction was mutual. Now it turns out I'm just being used as a patsy in some game you're playing to get out of your engagement.'

'Well—'

'Isn't that true?'

'Well, the way you put it makes it sound much worse than it is.'

'Yeah? Listen, buddy, it couldn't sound worse, because what you've just done is as worse as it gets. The only reason any dame wants a man to come on to her is because he's got the hots for her. Doing it for any other reason is just plain insulting. Can you get that into your thick skull? And can you also get out of my apartment—pronto!'

Blotto's slow brain added what he'd just done to the list, beginning with 'standing them up', of things women couldn't forgive. Oh, broken biscuits, they were a gender he'd just never understand.

*   *   *

When he stepped outside the apartment block, Blotto noticed, parked directly outside, a Cadillac limousine with darkened windows. He could just see the outline of the driver. The back door was open and two heavy-set men wearing double-breasted suits and carrying violin cases were standing by it.

'Hi,' said the larger one. 'We've come to take you for a ride.'

'Oh, that's frightfully decent of you,' said Blotto. 'There don't seem to be any taxis here for love nor money.'

141

18

A White Knight on a Mean Street

Twinks had never really worried about her brother's safety. Though his intellectual processes moved rather more slowly than her own, in the face of physical danger Blotto was infinitely resourceful. He thrived on the challenge of impossible odds. He loved defeating hordes of villains, preferably armed with nothing more than his faithful cricket bat.

But when he hadn't got back to Chapstick Towers by midday after his assignation with Choxy Mulligan, Twinks did suffer a rare moment of doubt. Had it perhaps not been entirely wise for her to encourage her brother to cosy up to the moll of one of Chicago's most notoriously jealous mobsters?

She was in her bedroom trying to come up with an answer to this dilemma when one of the Chapsticks' obsequious servants tapped on the door. On a silver salver he carried the brown envelope of a cablegram. Thinking it might be from Blotto, Twinks snatched the message up and opened it the moment the deliverer was out of the room.

Though not from her brother, it was from an equally welcome source. Professor Erasmus Holofernes. From his academic fastness in St Raphael's College, Oxford, the mighty brain had responded. And the length of his cabled message suggested that he was unworried by such worldly considerations as cost.

MY DEAR TWINKS, the message began, I APOLOGIZE FOR MY EXTREME TARDINESS IN RESPONDING TO YOUR MISSIVE. THIS WAS DUE TO MY GETTING ONE OF MY COLDS. AS YOU MAY BE AWARE, THOUGH OTHER PEOPLE DO GET COLDS, NONE OF THEM EVEN APPROACH THE SEVERITY OF THE ONES THAT AFFLICT ME. EVERY ORIFICE OF MY HEAD BECOMES EITHER STUFFED OR STREAMING AND I AM FORCED TO TAKE TO MY BED FOR SOMETIMES AS LONG AS A WEEK. WHEN I AM THUS AFFLICTED, I AM UNABLE TO UNDERTAKE EVEN THE SIMPLEST OF CHORES. AS A RESULT MY EXTENSIVE CORRESPONDENCE FROM CONTACTS AROUND THE WORLD GOES UNANSWERED AND BUILDS UP AN ENORMOUS BACKLOG. AND I AM UNABLE TO RESPOND EVEN TO MY FAVOURITE, MOST EMPATHETIC OF BRAINS—YOURS, TWINKS.

I HAVE CONSIDERED THE DILEMMA YOU APPRISED ME OF, AND THINK THE ONLY SOLUTION TO YOUR PROBLEMS WILL BE FOR YOUR BROTHER TO ABANDON HIS NORMALLY HONOURABLE MODE OF BEHAVIOUR AND DO SOMETHING THAT WILL LEAVE HIS PROSPECTIVE FATHER-IN-LAW NO CHOICE BUT TO END THE ENGAGEMENT. THE PRECISE NATURE OF WHAT IS DONE I LEAVE UP TO YOU AND YOUR EVER-FERTILE BRAIN, BUT IN THESE CIRCUMSTANCES A FAVOURED METHOD IS FOR THE MALE PARTY TO FORM A PUBLIC LIAISON WITH A WOMAN OF TOTALLY UNSUITABLE SOCIAL STANDING AND MORALITY.

Splendissimo, thought Twinks, great minds think alike.

NOW MY COLD HAS RECEDED, I AM OBVIOUSLY CONTACTABLE BY CABLEGRAM, SHOULD YOU WISH TO ENGAGE IN FURTHER DISCUSSION. IN THE EVENT THAT YOU NEED ON-THE-GROUND HELP, MY WIDE-REACHING STUDY OF CHICAGO HAS COME UP WITH THE NAME OF A PRIVATE INVESTIGATOR OF APPARENTLY INCORRUPTIBLE MORAL INTEGRITY, TO WHOM YOU MIGHT DIRECT YOUR ENQUIRIES. HIS NAME IS PAUL SIDNEY, AND HE HAS AN OFFICE ABOVE A DRY GOODS STORE AT NO 1752 BAY STREET. KEEP ME INFORMED ABOUT YOUR PROGRESS.

AND LET US MEET SOON. YOUR PRESENCE ALWAYS DOES ME GOOD. IT IS SO RARELY THAT I ENCOUNTER AN INTELLECT THAT EVEN DISTANTLY ASPIRES TO MATCH MY OWN. (BUT DON'T YOU DARE COME AND SEE ME IF YOU'VE GOT EVEN A VESTIGE OF A COLD!)

WITH THE FONDEST OF GOOD WISHES,
RAZZY.

The timing of his cablegram couldn't have been better. Twinks decided that, in the absence of Blotto, she might seek outside help. Using the lie that she wanted to investigate potential wedding outfits, she arranged for one of the Chapstick Towers chauffeurs to drive her into Chicago.

Once again she was unaware of the interest taken in her actions by the ever-observant Jimmy 'The Moose' Fettuchini. Nor did she know that, when Luther P. Chapstick III returned home later that morning from his assignation with the Dowager Duchess of Framlington, the bodyguard reported to him the news of Twinks breaking into his study.

She didn't hear the oaths sworn by her host as he was apprised of this news. Nor his vows to take revenge on the sister of his prospective son-in-law.

*　　*　　*

The November rain turned the sky the colour of dead auto tyres. Scraps of paper that might have blown about in the ferocious wind off Lake Michigan lay plastered to the sidewalk. The few people on the streets scuttled like crabs from the shelter of one awning to the next.

The Chapstick limousine stopped outside the dry goods store on Bay Street. The chauffeur was at first unwilling to leave Twinks alone in such a dubious neighbourhood, but a blast of the Dowager Duchess's manner from her daughter soon had him agreeing to pick her up from the same spot in an hour's time.

There were a few dull brass nameplates beside the door to the right of the dry goods store. They gave off an air of distant bankruptcy. Amongst them, secured by a rusted drawing pin, was a discoloured card printed with the words 'PAUL SIDNEY, PRIVATE INVESTIGATOR', beneath which had been scrawled in smudged ink, 'WALK ON UP'.

So Twinks walked on up.

The outer door of the office had a dusty glass panel printed in flaking gold with the name of some defunct law firm. The anteroom was cold like

145

stepping into a morgue. The dusty door to the inner office was ajar. Twinks tapped on it and a voice rasped out, 'Come in.'

Paul Sidney sat tipped back on a dusty swivel chair behind a dusty desk. All that stood on its surface was an ancient telephone, a half-empty bottle of scotch and a dusty toothglass in which two fingers of the hooch still remained. Blue-grey smoke spiralled lazily up from the cigarette hanging at the corner of his mouth. He was a trim man who looked after himself, but not quite enough. He wore a powder-blue shirt under a neat grey suit. His ice-blue eyes had seen a lot, not much of it pleasant.

'Hi,' he said without getting up from his chair. 'You're quite a dame. The kind the Pope might give up Lent for.' He gestured to a depressed cracking leather armchair. 'Sit. Tell me what gives.'

'I'm worried,' Twinks said as she sat, 'that my brother may have been the victim of criminal activity.'

'He's here in Chicago?'

'Yes.'

'Then you're right, lady. Everyone in Chicago is the victim of criminal activity. Even the ones who perpetrate the criminal activity. City's a swamphole full of rats. And the biggest fattest rats are the ones supposed to be on the side of law and order. Tell me about your brother.'

Twinks gave him a brief résumé of Blotto's last twenty-four hours.

'Then he's either stupid or mad,' said Paul Sidney. 'Sweet-talking Spagsy Chiaparelli's broad is like smothering yourself in honey and then poking a burning stick into a beehive. Chiaparelli's one

146

jealous guy.'

'So you think Spagsy's got Blotto?'

'I'd say that's for sure. Spagsy runs this town like his own toy railroad. There's no pie in Chicago that ain't got a portion of Spagsy's finger in it. I'd say most likely by now your brother's in the lake wearing dandy cement footwear.'

'That'd never happen to Blotto,' Twinks protested.

'Why not?'

'Because he'd never stand still long enough for the cement to set. Whatever kind of gluepot he gets into, Blotto always manages to escape.'

'Dream on, doll. Chicago ain't no city for idealists. Though I too have ideals. I dream of a time when I can step out on the sidewalk and not be confronted by a pug with a rod. I dream of a time when the police try to catch the crooks rather than drinking illegal hooch with them. I'm a man of dreams. A man of grey, scorched dreams. And though most of them have been squished like ladybugs on the windshield of a car, I still have a few. What's your name, lady?'

'Twinks.'

'You were christened that?'

'I was christened Honoria Charlotte Victoria Ermintrude Delauncey Lyminster.'

'I'll call you Twinks.'

'I am the daughter of the late Duke of Tawcester.'

He nodded, unimpressed. Maybe he regarded the aristocracy as just another manifestation of injustice.

'Well, look, Mr Sidney—'

'Call me Paul.'

'Paul, I want to employ you to find my brother.'

'Don't waste your sugar. You'd be whistling in the wind.'

'Are you not looking for work?' Twinks gestured round the bare dusty office. 'Doesn't look like you have too much of it.'

'I get by.'

'What are your rates?'

'Hundred bucks down. Then it's per day. And mileage for the Packard.'

Before he had finished speaking a crisp green note had been removed from the reticule and was on the table in front of him. 'You're employed,' said Twinks.

The private eye nodded slowly. 'You've persuaded me. Just let's get one thing clear. You're a classy broad and I dare say you've been told that many times. But I ain't taking your sugar because you're a classy broad. I'm taking the job because, even in a hellhole like Chicago, I believe justice must survive. It's gotta reach the light of day, just like flowers come up in the cracks between the slabs on the sidewalk.'

'I'm not arguing with any of that,' said Twinks. 'One thing . . . do you work on your own?'

'Sure,' Paul Sidney replied. 'I'm alone on the street. I don't carry a gun. The only weapon I'm tooled up with is my integrity.'

'Except this time,' said Twinks, 'you're not working alone.'

'But I need to,' he objected. 'I need to be alone. One dark figure on the dark street, fedora crammed down over my eyes, collar of my coat turned up against the rain. That's me. A loner. Of course I work on my own.'

148

Twinks shook her head. 'This time you're working with me.'

For a moment he looked like he was going to disagree. But feeling the full impact of one of the Dowager Duchess's basilisk stares from his client's eyes, he didn't argue.

19

Blotto and the Mob

The evening before Twinks's encounter with Paul Sidney, things were not going too well for her brother. Even someone with Blotto's slow perception didn't take long to realize that the men who'd hustled him into the Cadillac limousine were unlikely to be taking him straight to a reunion with his beloved Lagonda. He picked up clues from their manner, which did not indicate a spirit of co-operation. Like the gun whose barrel the one on the back seat kept dug into his ribs.

But though he asked in the politest way where they were actually taking him, they proved to be distinctly uninformative on that subject. Indeed he found himself wondering whether they could actually speak at all. All of their instructions to him had taken the form of grunts rather than words. Mind you, supported by gestures from their guns, they were very articulate grunts.

Nor could he get many clues as to their route and destination from the outside world. The Cadillac seemed quickly to have left the city lights behind and they were driving out into unrelenting darkness.

'It's as black as a mole's armpit,' Blotto observed at one point, but this attempt to engage his captors in conversation proving ineffective, he didn't bother again.

At last the car seemed to slow down and heavy jolting about suggested that it had left the main thoroughfare to join some rougher, cross-country route. Then the Cadillac stopped.

The driver didn't move, nor did he switch off the engine. Whatever was about to happen wasn't expected to last long.

The two heavies in the back manhandled Blotto out of the limousine. But the barrel of the gun one held didn't for a moment slacken its pressure on his ribs.

It was as dark as pitch. The wind slapped cold rain on to his face. As his eyes accommodated, he could see that they were miles from anywhere. The only sign of human interference with bleak nature was a high barn, suggesting that they were perhaps on farmland.

The two heavies pinioning his arms were speaking now, and in more than grunts.

'I say we just ice him, Rat Teeth,' said the one with the gun. Then with an evil laugh, he asked their prisoner, 'Howdja like the idea of icing?'

It seemed an odd, rather out-of-context question, but Blotto had long ceased expecting logical discourse from Americans. 'Well, I like it on a Christmas cake,' he replied.

Ignoring him, the other heavy objected, 'Icing wasn't in the orders, Two Legs.'

'Who needs orders? We was told to "take him for a ride". Every other time Vic "Rat Teeth"

Papardelle and Michael "Two Legs" Conchiglioni have been told to take someone for a ride we've iced them.'

'Maybe. But the Boss is getting antsy these days. You know how he likes to keep all the book-keeping neat. Lemmy "The Hook" Vermicelli—he iced some boofer without checking. The Boss iced him.'

'So what you saying, Rat Teeth? We lock the bozo in the barn, we go back into the city, we find the Boss, we say to him, "You want that dingle iced?" He says, "Sure I do. I told you to take him for a ride, didn't I?" Then suddenly it's us the boss is antsy with.'

'Two Legs, I still think it's worth checking,' maintained Vic 'Rat Teeth' Papardelle.

'But nobody's going to miss this chimp. He's English, for God's sake. I say we ice him,' insisted Michael 'Two Legs' Conchiglioni.

As their discussion continued, for the first time that evening Blotto's natural optimism was clouded by the thought that he might be in serious danger. Danger itself didn't worry him, indeed he rather relished it. But if his life was going to end in that harsh wet landscape, perhaps he should give a little thought to his own mortality.

The little thought didn't take long. Having been brought up Church of England, his attitude to religion was rather vague. The chaplain at Eton had certainly mentioned some kind of afterlife, though he hadn't given much detail about its specifics.

Anyway, forget the afterlife, there were things about his current life that Blotto reckoned he'd miss. Cricket, obviously ... Hunting ... Solving mysteries with Twinks ... Yes, he'd probably miss that most.

But then again, being 'iced' in a blighted field in Illinois would provide a perfect solution to the Mary Chapstick problem. She couldn't marry someone dead. Blotto had to admit that there were arguments on both sides of the 'icing' dilemma.

He was still mightily relieved that Vic 'Rat Teeth' Papardelle's view prevailed over that of Michael 'Two Legs' Conchiglioni, and for the time being the two heavies agreed to lock Blotto in the barn while they went to consult the Boss about his fate. It was only a temporary reprieve, but at least it was a reprieve. And the dilapidated state of the barn's exterior suggested that breaking out of it would not present too much of a problem for a young man at the peak of his fitness. Optimism flooded back along Blotto's arteries.

It swelled even more when he realized that his captors were not going to truss him up but leave him free to wander at will around the barn. They even put a light on for him. How generous. Short of clapping him heartily on the shoulder and saying, 'Feel free to escape when you want to,' they couldn't have done much more.

He waited until the sounds of the departing Cadillac had become lost in the wind that whistled through the barn and then he started looking for the holes through which it whistled, confident of finding one that was Blotto-sized. Failing that, there was bound to be a rotting door or cracked window through which he could make his getaway. Then, as soon as possible, he would be reunited with Twinks and hear the good news of the effect his supposed dalliance with Choxy Mulligan had had on Luther P. Chapstick III. His engagement to

152

Mary was virtually over already!

But after half an hour of circling the interior walls, pressing and probing every now and then to find a weakness, he was forced to admit that he had somewhat underestimated the efficiency of Spagsy Chiaparelli's mobsters. The barn was sealed as tight as a limpet on a rock. Despite its exterior dilapidation, a metal shell had been constructed inside the building. The only entrance was the double doors through which he had been frogmarched in and, though they had wooden cladding, their main structure was of solid steel. What was more, their locks held firm. The barn had been fortified as if anticipating an imminent machine-gun attack (which, when Blotto came to think about the subject, it probably was).

Frustrated in his attempts to find an escape route, he started to explore the contents of the barn, hoping to find something with which to break out or defend himself.

There were certainly plenty of weapons there. Along one whole wall stood racks of machine guns, rifles and pistols, enough to terrorize the whole city of Chicago (which was of course what they were for). But, annoyingly, each firearm was locked into its individual holder and no amount of pulling and manoeuvring could dislodge it. And the boxes of ammunition nearby were locked and chained together.

Against another wall were piled great towers of barrels. The smell that emanated from the occasional spillage made it clear that they contained alcohol. Blotto contemplated fortifying himself with a snifter and cupped a hand under one dripping leak. But as the first drip stripped off a couple of layers of skin he whipped his hand away. He had no idea what the rotgut was made from, but didn't envy the people who were going to be drinking it.

The wall opposite the doors didn't have much clutter against it. There was just a low-sitting handcart, whose contents were covered by some old sacks. Blotto moved cautiously across and lifted the sacking to reveal about thirty large ingots of gold bullion. On each was stamped: 'PROPERTY OF U.S. GOVERNMENT'. For the first time he began to get some sense of the scale of Spagsy Chiaparelli's operation.

The space at the centre of the barn was dominated by three large and one slightly smaller boxlike structures covered with tarpaulins. Their outlines were familiar and as Blotto removed the sheeting from the first he was not surprised to uncover another Cadillac limousine. Tools and metal components were scattered around and underneath the car, and for a moment Blotto couldn't work out what was being done to it. But kneeling down and exploring beneath the chassis provided the answer quickly enough.

A new compartment was being attached to the underbelly of the limo. It was accessed from a hidden trapdoor in front of the back seats. The space inside was big enough to hide from prying eyes at least three barrels of the firewater. Or two men. Or two bodies.

Blotto shuddered slightly as he moved across to check out under the other two large tarpaulins. Though the work hadn't progressed quite as far as on the first limo, the same kind of conversion job was being done there too.

He crossed to the smallest of the covered shapes and as he slipped back the sheeting a surge of joy ran through his entire body. Though he doubted whether that had been their main intention, Rat Teeth and Two Legs had reunited him with his precious Lagonda!

So excited was he by the sight of those beautiful familiar lines that he didn't hear the doors to the barn open. He wasn't aware of anything until he heard a cold voice behind him saying, 'So we meet again, you English scumdouche!'

He turned to find himself facing Spagsy Chiaparelli, flanked by Vic 'Rat Teeth' Papardelle and Michael 'Two Legs' Conchiglioni. The harsh light accentuated the scar that cut across the Boss's face. There was no hint of compassion in his granite features. Or indeed of any other emotion.

All three men nursed Tommy guns in the crooks of their pinstriped arms.

20

Deliverance!

Still ignorant of her brother's fate, Twinks continued the investigation with her new sidekick. Paul Sidney had a network of contacts throughout Chicago. With Twinks still there in the office, he rang through to a police lieutenant who had been bought by Spagsy Chiaparelli. The cop in question knew (and did nothing about) everything that went on in the mobster's world. The man confirmed that Blotto had been 'taken for a ride'. He didn't hold out any hopes of Twinks ever seeing her brother again alive—or probably, knowing the efficiency of Spagsy's clean-up operations, dead either.

'I know he's all right,' Twinks persisted. 'If something murdey'd happened to him, I'd feel it in my marrow.'

The P.I. chuckled mirthlessly. He stood up from the swivel chair, downed the remains of his scotch, took his trench-coat down from a rack and crammed the fedora on his head. 'Let's get out on the mean streets,' he said. 'See what gives. And hope we find something other than a corpse.'

*   *   *

'You been sugar-talking my dame!' Spagsy Chiaparelli spat the words out at Blotto. 'No boofer who does that wakes up the next morning!' The Boss jerked his head back to the open doors behind him. 'Get out there!'

'Why?' asked Blotto, reasonably enough.

''Cause I ain't gonna mess my floor with your blood.'

Blotto thought he saw a rather clever escape route. 'And what if I don't move out there?'

'Then I do mess my floor with your blood.'

Oh well, it had been worth trying, thought Blotto as he moved past the three hoods into the darkness. His gait was deliberately slow, but the minute he got past the doors he was determined to break into the kind of sprinting for which his Eton records for the One-Hundred- and Two-Hundred-Yard Dashes still stood. Though the odds were still against him, he reckoned he was in with a chance.

But before he could take the first step, the

headlights from two limousines outside snapped on, dazzling him. When, after a couple of seconds, he could see again, he was aware of a semicircle of Chiaparelli gangsters standing in the field around the doorway. Each had a Tommy gun.

Oh, broken biscuits, thought Blotto. The odds against him had suddenly shortened by quite a lot.

'You want us to do a colander job on him, Boss?' asked Vic 'Rat Teeth' Papardelle. 'All shoot at once, perforate him proper so he tears neatly along the dotted lines?'

'No,' snarled Spagsy Chiaparelli. 'Anyone who tries to slip Choxy the sweets I ice myself.'

Blotto was aware of the sound of an approaching car and saw headlights flickering about as it tackled the rough road to the barn. 'Be careful, Mr Chiaparelli!' he cried out, 'It's the police!'

'So? What are they going to do? You forget I own the police.'

'Oh, so you do,' said Blotto, remembering the authorities' corpse-clearing cooperation the previous night.

But Spagsy did at least defer icing him until he'd seen who was in the arriving limo. Blotto was, however, under no illusion that it would be a long reprieve.

The long vehicle came to a halt, its headlights also trained on him. The driver kept the engine running. Out of the back stepped Jimmy 'The Moose' Fettuchini and Toni 'Nostrils' Linguini, followed by Luther P. Chapstick III.

'What gives here, Spagsy?' asked the cattle baron.

'This scumdouche is about to get iced.'

Chapstick raised a hand. 'No.'

'Whaddya mean, "no"?'

'This scumdouche is about to marry my daughter.'

'Listen, the chimp tried to cornswiggle my broad.'

'Forget it. Mary needs him alive.'

'And woddif I say I don't care what Mary wants.'

'I say the understanding you and I have stops being an understanding.'

Chapstick's words did seem to give Spagsy Chiaparelli pause. 'Luther, our understanding's good. Together we cover the waterfront, all fine and dandy. All of Chicago and maybe soon we add New York to the mix. It's a good understanding. We don't want to put that at risk over me icing some voidbrain.'

'This particular voidbrain is the one I want to marry my daughter.'

'You want your daughter to marry a dingle who tries to cornswiggle another man's dame?'

'Deveroox doesn't even know what cornswiggling is.' That at least, thought Blotto, is entirely true. 'He's as innocent as a baby,' the cattle baron went on. 'Slipping the sweets to Choxy was his sister's idea. She thought it might make me not want him as a son-in-law.'

Now how did Luther P. Chapstick III know that? Blotto wondered.

Anyway, his arguments seemed to be having their effect on Spagsy Chiaparelli. Reluctantly the mobster lowered his Tommy gun. 'I don't like doing this, Luther,' he complained, 'but if it's going to affect our understanding . . .'

'Sure it is. And don't forget I put you on to the government bullion trucks. I didn't do that, we

158

wouldn't have our little stash in the barn here, would we? And we wouldn't have the happy future we've worked out for ourselves, would we?'

Spagsy Chiaparelli nodded slowly. 'You right.' He looked wistfully at Blotto. 'Just feels bad to me when I say I'm going to ice someone and I don't ice 'em.'

Blotto thought perhaps it was the moment for him to say something. 'I really don't mind,' he ventured.

'Tell you what, Spagsy,' said Chapstick magnanimously. 'If Deveroox ever treats Mary bad, if he ever tries again to get out of their engagement or cornswiggles another broad when they're actually married . . . I hand him over to you for icing. Can't say fairer than that, can I? Is it a deal.'

After a long moment Spagsy Chiaparelli nodded. The two men shook hands.

Luther P. Chapstick III nodded. 'Get him in the limo.'

Jimmy 'The Moose' Fettuchini and Toni 'Nostrils' Linguini stepped forward, but Blotto didn't need an escort. He was quite happy—and actually felt rather relieved—to be getting into the Chapstick Towers car.

So he didn't hear his prospective father-in-law lean across to Chiaparelli and whisper, 'But, Spagsy, if you're still feeling bad about not having someone to ice, find Deveroox's sister. She's more trouble than a kettle full of scorpions. You have my permission to ice her any day you want.'

21

The White Knight Errant

Luther P. Chapstick III was silent as the limousine drove them back to Chapstick Towers. So were Jimmy 'The Moose' Fettuchini and Toni 'Nostrils' Linguini. They were a good ten minutes into the journey before Blotto realized that his Lagonda was still in the barn. The urge to suggest they return to reclaim it was only momentary. Even someone of Blotto's limited intellectual powers could recognize that he'd had a lucky escape from being iced. And further irritating the hypersensitive Spagsy Chiaparelli would just be asking for trouble.

He wondered if he would ever see the Lagonda again.

The thought that he wouldn't plunged him into another cold bath of gloom. Twinks's plan for him to escape the clutches of Mary Chapstick by slipping the sweets to Choxy Mulligan had been completely blown out of the water. And since she'd been so atypically slow coming up with that scheme, he wasn't over-optimistic about her devising another before the dreadful shutter of his impending marriage slammed down.

He couldn't wait to see Twinks again. Even if she couldn't offer him a practical solution, she would at least commiserate with his wretchedness.

*   *   *

Paul Sidney and Twinks had pounded the mean

streets of Chicago all evening trying to find information about her brother, but without success. The bums in the gutters knew nothing, the good-time girls in the doorways drew blanks, and the speakeasy barkeeps shook their heads. Wearily the two investigators trudged their way back to the Bay Street office.

The cold rain stung their cheeks like pellets of lead. Heavy clouds blanketed the Windy City, but without the warmth of blankets. The only light came from the small flickering glow of Paul Sidney's integrity.

Inside the office he hung their dripping coats on the rack, reached into a filing cabinet for the scotch bottle and two grubby glasses. Wordlessly he poured a handful of fingers into each and passed one across to Twinks. She sipped it gratefully.

'Sorry,' said Paul Sidney.

'Sorry? Why?'

'That your brother's not to be found.'

'Oh, he's to be found. We just haven't found him yet.'

'People who cross Spagsy Chiaparelli don't get found.'

'It'll be different with Blotto.'

Sidney moved across to look out of the dusty window at the back of his office. Not much of a view. Small yard barely big enough to stab a punk in. Broken furniture, broken dreams. Enough rainwater to wash it dirty.

'Lousy place,' he said, 'but somebody owns it. Somebody screws rent for it out of me and other sad goons who've ended up here. Somebody owns everything. Somebody owns everyone. A very few fat rich men own all the others. And no one lifts a finger to stop them. That's how the game is played. Always has been. It's hard for a man to keep faith in a world like that, but it's the only one we've got.'

After a long, long silence he said, 'You don't wear a wedding ring.'

'No,' Twinks agreed. 'In England you have to have a husband to get one of them. I don't have one.'

'I bet a lot of men have asked you.'

'Maybe. Have you been married, Mr Sidney?'

'There've been women.'

'I didn't doubt it.'

'But some want too much and some don't want enough.'

'And what do you want?' asked Twinks.

'I don't want to compromise. Anywhere in my life. So if I don't find the perfect dame, I'd rather stay alone. It hurts, but not as bad as hurting someone else.'

Twinks was silent, wondering how long he could keep this circuitous monologue going.

Quite a lot longer, it seemed. 'Anyway,' he went on, 'what are the chances of meeting someone perfect in Chicago? Everyone here is corroded by the rust of despair. The blight of disappointment. The running sores of corruption. Hard to achieve perfection in a hellhole like this.'

Again she couldn't think of any relevant comment.

'You're a dame who looks perfect, Twinks. Maybe we could play sad jazz together for a while.'

'I rather doubt it,' she said, aggrieved at being commandeered into his fantasy.

'No, you're right. It wouldn't last.'

'It wouldn't last because it wouldn't start,' said

Twinks tartly.

He nodded, a little ruefully. 'Probably better that way. Dames like to have men's full attention. They never get that with me. A part of my mind is always thinking about injustice.'

'No woman would be very keen on playing second fiddle to injustice.'

'No. I guess that's why, with all the dames I meet, nothing lasts very long.'

'It could be one of the reasons,' Twinks agreed.

'But is justice such a lot to ask for? With all the dames who fall for me—'

Mercifully, so far as Twinks was concerned, the private investigator was interrupted by the ringing of the telephone.

He snatched it up. 'Sidney.' Immediately recognizing the voice at the other end of the line, he asked, 'What gives? Uh-huh. Uh-huh. Uh-huh. Uh-huh. Uh-huh? Uh-*huh*!'

He slammed the receiver down in its cradle and sprang back to the window. 'Informant of mine. He says Spagsy's boys're coming here!'

'What have you done to upset him?'

'It's not me they're after. It's you!'

'How do they know I'm here?'

'That barkeep, Freddie "The Cheese and Tomato" Macaroni, must've blabbed.'

Downing the remains of her scotch and picking up her reticule, Twinks announced, 'I'd better get out of here as quick as a lizard's lick!'

'No time,' said Paul Sidney, looking down from the window to the yard below. 'They're coming in the back way.' He looked round in panic.

'What about that cupboard?' suggested Twinks.

'Cupboard?' echoed the private investigator.

Remembering she was in a foreign country, Twinks said, 'Closet.'

'Good thinking,' he said, bustling her in, throwing her coat after her and locking the door.

He just had time to slip her scotch glass into the filing cabinet and raise his to his lips as he sank in his swivel chair, when the office door was forced open by the considerable bulk of Vic 'Rat Teeth' Papardelle and Michael 'Two Legs' Conchiglioni. They had foregone the formality of violin cases and just held naked Tommy guns.

'So, Mr Sidney,' growled Vic 'Rat Teeth' Papardelle, 'we meet again.'

'So we do,' said Paul Sidney coolly. He had just lit up, and let out a little cloud of cigarette smoke. He watched it melt in the rather dim light of the office.

'I still ain't forgiven you for having Giovanni "Glass Eye" Campanelle canned.'

The private investigator shrugged. 'He took out Luigi "Kneecaps" Farfalloni. He was lucky to escape the noose.'

'Yeah, but that was Mob business. No need to get the cops and the judiciary involved.'

'I'm sorry,' Paul Sidney replied, with a note of nobility in his voice. 'I can't see injustice without wanting to get it replaced by justice.'

'In this city that's the way to end up dead,' said Vic 'Rat Teeth' Papardelle.

'Risk I have to take.' Paul Sidney let another stream of bluish cigarette smoke lose itself in the darkness above him.

'Anyway,' Michael 'Two Legs' Conchiglioni interrupted brusquely, 'we ain't here to talk about dead cases, Sidney. Spagsy Chiaparelli reckons you've got something he wants.'

'I wonder what that might be ...?' Then the private investigator suggested, 'Honesty?'

'Don't come the wise guy with me,' said Michael 'Two Legs' Conchiglioni, waving a threatening Tommy gun, 'or you'll be eating a lead breakfast. Spagsy don't like jokes. Remember, when Dino "The Blini" Strozzapreti told him the one about the salesman and the farmer's daughter? Spagsy iced him. Anyway, let's cut the cackle. Spagsy says you've been seen around the city with some English frail called Twinks.'

'What if I have?'

'Spagsy wants her.'

'What for?'

'That's Spagsy's business.'

'I think it might be my business too. Suppose he wanted her for immoral purposes ... or to do her some harm ... well, I don't know whether my conscience would allow me to hand her over ... that is if I even knew where she was.'

'Sure you know,' rasped Vic 'Rat Teeth' Papardelle. 'Freddie "The Cheese and Tomato" Macaroni said he'd seen you with her less than an hour ago.'

'An hour's a long time. Plenty for a dame to leave my company. Many've done it quicker. If you want the truth, this frail called Twinks has gone back to where she's staying. Which ...' Paul Sidney grinned sardonically '... and I'll give you this information for free, is old Luther P. Chapstick III's place.'

'If she's gone back there,' said Michael 'Two Legs' Conchiglioni, 'our job's done. It was Chapstick who told Spagsy he wanted her iced.'

In the breathheld silence of her cupboard (or rather closet—though it still felt like a cupboard to her) Twinks was shocked by this news, but she managed not to let out a gasp of surprise.

'Well,' said Sidney, 'I guess you go and check things out at Chapstick Towers.'

'Yeah, maybe that's what we should do,' said Michael 'Two Legs' Conchiglioni.

His partner wasn't convinced 'This dingle might be saying that to put us off the scent.' Without asking permission, Vic 'Rat Teeth' Papardelle picked up the phone on the desk and asked for the Chapstick number. When he got through he barked out a series of questions, then replaced the mouthpiece on its cradle.

'Just talked to Jimmy "The Moose" Fettuchini,' he announced. 'No sign of the girl there, though her mug of a brother's returned safely.'

In the cupboard/closet Twinks restrained a 'Larksissimo!' of triumph and vindication.

'So,' Vic 'Rat Teeth' Papardelle continued, 'she ain't there, and I still think you know where she is, Sidney, and I think we can persuade you to give us that information.' Both he and Michael 'Two Legs' Conchiglioni raised their Tommy guns menacingly to their shoulders.

Paul Sidney chuckled. 'OK, you blow me away— where does that get you? Dead mouths don't spill many beans.'

'No, but if maybe we hurt you a little ...? "Two Legs" is famous for the fretwork he does with his blade. Maybe there's bits of you that could do with a bit of fancy carving ...?'

'You can try.' Paul Sidney rolled up a sleeve of

166

his jacket and shirt, exposing his forearm. 'Like to start your artwork there, would you?' Michael 'Two Legs' Conchiglioni looked at his mate for permission while the private investigator went on, 'But I'd better warn you, I'll die before my mouth gets unclammed. So it'll be just like you blown me away.'

'Yeah,' agreed Michael 'Two Legs' Conchiglioni, putting down his Tommy gun and producing a wicked-looking knife from a hidden shoulder-sheath, 'but I might have more fun going the pretty way.'

Another shrug from Paul Sidney. 'Do it whichever way you want. You'll still get nothing.'

Conchiglioni looked lovingly at his blade, then once again appealed to Papardelle, who shook his head. 'We ain't tried offering him the mazuma yet.'

Paul Sidney laughed out loud. 'Well, if you think I can be bought, then—'

'Every man has his price,' said Vic 'Rat Teeth' Papardelle, taking a roll of greenbacks out of his trouser pocket and detaching a couple. 'Two grand says you tell us where the girl is.'

'No, it doesn't. It just tells me what a low-rent pair of grifters you are.'

Three more notes were unrolled. 'Five grand.'

Another harsh laugh. 'You got the wrong man. Five grand might buy you a run-down cop with an eel juice problem. It don't buy Paul Sidney.'

Five more greenbacks were added to the proffering hand. 'Ten grand. How many days snooping would it take you to pull in that much?'

'That's not really the question. After a day's snooping I can at least look at my face in the mirror.'

Vic 'Rat Teeth' Papardelle unrolled a lot more notes. 'Fifty grand. I bet you never even seen that amount of money.'

'No, and I wouldn't want to . . . not unless I knew for sure that the notes were clean. And I don't figure anything that's spent any time in your pocket is anywhere near clean.'

The unrolling of notes continued. So did Vic 'Rat Teeth' Papardelle. 'Like I said, every man has his price.' He patted the dollars into a neat brick. 'You tell me where that frail Twinks is, Mr Sidney, and I give you a hundred grand. How's about that?'

'Ah, now you're talking,' said the private investigator, leaning across to scoop up the money. 'She's in the closet.'

22

Twinks in Peril!

'We got the girl,' said Spagsy Chiaparelli on the telephone to Chapstick Towers. 'What you want we do with her?'

'Take her for a ride. She's trouble.' The meat-packing magnate looked viciously from his desk across the November expanse of Lake Michigan.

'Don't you need her for the wedding? If Mary's marrying her brother?'

'No, better she takes a powder. The boy's a bozo, he'll do what he's told. The sister's got brains, though. Moose told me she been snooping around my study. Copied some documents about a little plan I have to deal with the Katzenjammers once and for all. Like I say, she's trouble.'

'So I ice her?'

'You ice her.'

'You got it. Moving on to the New York business . . .'

Luther P. Chapstick III was instantly alert. 'Yeah?'

'Hit a bit of rough water there.'

'Whaddya mean? The deal's still on?'

'It's on for the moment. But Harry "Three Bananas" Pennoni's getting a bit antsy about his payment. Wants it within forty-eight hours or the deal's off.'

'So we get it to him within forty-eight hours. Where's the problem?'

'The problem is that the New York cops don't toe the line like they do here in Chicago.'

'Sounds like Harry "Three Bananas" Pennoni ain't doing his job.'

'Too right he ain't. That's why we want to get in there. Give me coupla months, we'll have them like the Chicago cops—all lapdogs. But at the moment there's some new palooka in charge of New York's finest. He's been doing sneaky stuff like getting the licence plates of all the autos we run, even getting mugshots of my oppos.'

'What you telling me, Spagsy?'

'I'm telling you if any of my regular goons runs the payment down to the Big Apple, there's a serious danger the New York cops might spot the plate or the noseframe and head them off before they get to Harry "Three Bananas" Pennoni.'

'So what do we do?'

'Best thing we could do is find some patsy whose

record's as blank as a hooker's conscience. We get him driving some wheels that aren't on the cops' lists. He takes the stuff to Pennoni.'

'You got some chimp in mind?'

'No. Work I do means most of my acquaintances do have the odd blot on their records. Thought you might know someone . . .? Needs to be a real bozo, kinda dingle who'd never realize he was being set up.'

At that moment the door to Luther P. Chapstick III's study opened. A bark of 'Come in!' admitted Blotto. A smile spread over the cattle baron's stony features. 'You know, Spagsy,' he said, 'I think I might have the perfect person. I'll call you back.'

After he'd replaced the mouthpiece, he positively beamed at his prospective son-in-law. 'Well, Deveroox,' he asked, 'what can I do for you?'

'I was just wondering, Mr Chapstick . . .'

'Luther, please . . .' came the reply, an informality that hadn't been offered before.

'I was wondering if you knew any way I could get my Lagonda back . . .?'

'Do you know, son,' replied Luther P. Chapstick III, his voice dripping with bonhomie, 'I think I know the perfect way.'

*   *   *

Expecting Spagsy Chiaparelli, Choxy Mulligan looked up at her apartment door when she heard the key in the lock. To her surprise three people walked in—Vic 'Rat Teeth' Papardelle and Michael 'Two Legs' Conchiglioni, frogmarching a reluctant-looking Twinks.

'What's this about?' asked Choxy.

170

'The Boss wants you to look after this dame for a while,' said Papardelle.

'Oh?'

'He's busy icing some dingle who's two-handed him in one of his gambling joints. He'll pick up the girl when he's shot of that.'

'That is,' said Twinks with patrician *froideur*, 'if I am still here.'

'You'll still be here,' Michael 'Two Legs' Conchiglioni assured her. 'No escape from this place, is there, Choxy?'

With a note of wistfulness in her voice, the singer agreed that there wasn't. For a moment Twinks wondered how voluntary Choxy Mulligan's consorting with Spagsy Chiaparelli was. Any weakness in the woman, any resentment about being owned by the *capo dei capi* might be something Twinks could work on to effect an escape.

'Listen, lady,' said Conchiglioni, 'there's no way outta here. And there's no way outta what the Boss has in mind for you. Apart from Boggy "Two Noses" Taormina downstairs on the main entrance, you'll have me and "Two Legs" outside the door on the landing. Get used to it, doll—you're going to be here till the Boss gets back.'

'You mentioned,' said Twinks coolly, ' "what the Boss has in mind for me". Am I going to be allowed to know what that is?'

Michael 'Two Legs' Conchiglioni let out a laugh like blood going down an abattoir drain, while his associate replied grimly, 'You'll find out soon enough.'

*   *   *

171

Blotto's steam-rollered spirits did lift a little the following morning at the sight of his Lagonda on the Chapstick Towers drive. Being behind the wheel of that little baby could not fail to give him a brief respite from gloomy thoughts of marriage. And at least a 1,500-mile round-trip to New York would keep him at a distance from the pathetic adoration of Mary Chapstick. (Mind you, she had insisted that he should call her as soon as he arrived in New York, and reluctantly he had promised to do so.)

He knew the excursion would be only a temporary respite, but he really relished the prospect of driving on the open road (even if it would be on the wrong side of it).

What was more, in the Lagonda's dickey he'd found his precious cricket bat, still safe and sound. After a reverential stroke and sniff of its battered linseed-oil-scented surface, he stood it up in the car's front seat like an honoured passenger.

So it was in more cheerful mood that Blotto drove the Lagonda down the Chapstick Towers drive on his way to New York. And that mood improved considerably when he got on to the main highway. So preoccupied was he with the pleasure of driving that he didn't notice the small black Chevrolet that had joined his route a few miles from Chapstick Towers and continued doggedly to stay some two or three cars behind the Lagonda.

*   *   *

In his office, which was the entire top floor of the Chainey Hotel, Spagsy Chiaparelli was thoughtful. His plans were going well. He'd averted a falling-out

172

with Luther P. Chapstick III over icing the English duke and he had his mitts on the boofer's sister, who was reckoned to be by far the more intelligent and dangerous of the siblings. So pretty soon her chitterlings'd be griddled.

Meanwhile her brother was playing the perfect patsy, acting as messenger between the criminal families of Chicago and New York. He was such a boneheaded swell that, even if the cops did stop him, they'd never suspect him of washing his hands in dirty water.

On the other hand ... Spagsy Chiaparelli was always very anxious about security. The fewer people there were who knew about his activities, the cosier he slept at night. And even though this Devereux dingle seemed too stupid to spot a buzzard in a beehive, he might still blab something to someone. Better safe than sorry ...

Sure, Luther P. Chapstick III might be a bit soured off to hear his daughter's fiancé had been chilled, but no suspicion would be attached to Spagsy, the bosom buddy with whom he had such a great 'understanding'. The two of them would continue to run Chicago—and soon New York— together. The duke-erasing job would be done by some goon in the Big Apple. Nothing to do with the Chicago operation.

Kill the messenger, thought Spagsy, always a good safety measure. He picked up the telephone, placed a call to Harry 'Three Bananas' Pennoni and gave his instructions.

23

Blotto in Peril!

Blotto wasn't entirely happy with the way the Lagonda was handling. Normally he drove it like he rode Mephistopheles. It was hard to detect where man stopped and car or horse began. But on the 700-mile drive to New York the beloved Lagonda didn't feel like its usual self. It seemed to lack that huge pick-up of acceleration he so treasured. It felt heavier and less secure on cornering.

Blotto wished he could just take the thing down to the Tawcester Towers garages and let Corky Froggett have a look at it. The chauffeur tuned that engine like a maestro tuned a Stradivarius.

The thought reminded Blotto of his current situation. There was a really strong chance that he would never see Corky Froggett again. Never see Tawcester Towers again either. Spend the rest of his life driving on the wrong side of the road and watching rounders . . .

Oh, biscuits smashed to smithereens, thought Blotto miserably.

*　　　*　　　*

Ziggy 'Tomato Sauce' Radiatore was the best hitman in New York and he knew it. He'd never bothered counting his victims, he didn't suffer from that kind of ostentatious pride. Who cared about numbers? For Ziggy 'Tomato Sauce' Radiatore, knowing he was the best was good enough.

He was lying on a sheetless mattress in his undecorated apartment when the call came through from Harry 'Three Bananas' Pennoni.

He was given the target's name, the marque and number of the vehicle he'd be driving and his estimated arrival time in a Little Italy garage. Early evening the following day. The money would be the usual, paid into the usual account. The call ended.

Ziggy 'Tomato Sauce' Radiatore unlocked the arsenal of guns that lay in a steel box under his bed. In turn he caressed them lovingly, decided which one he would use to whack the Englishman.

*   *   *

'My brother told me that, when it comes to singing, you're absolutely the lark's larynx,' said Twinks.

'That's nice of him,' said Choxy Mulligan. 'He seems like a nice guy . . . apart from . . .'

'I'm so sorry. I'm absolutely crabwhacked about what we did. We were so obsessed with getting Blotto out of his engagement that we didn't consider your feelings.'

'Feelings?' drawled Choxy. 'I'm not so sure I have feelings. Or if I did have some, Spagsy's seen to it that they've been encased in cement— one of his favourite ways of dealing with anything inconvenient.'

The two women were sitting cosily over a pot of tea.

Twinks picked up the conversation. 'From what you say that stencher Spagsy doesn't seem to treat you very well.'

The singer shrugged. 'He buys me stuff. Jewellery . . . this fancy apartment . . . He beats up

175

on me too, but that's guys, isn't it? I don't have too much cause for complaint.'

'Does he ever ask your advice?'

'Spagsy? Ask my advice? What the hell would he want to do that for?'

'To show that he respects you as a woman.'

'What?' Choxy Mulligan burst out into rich, husky laughter. 'Hell, where I come from no woman gets respect. We get bought, we get used, we get beat up on, we get cheated on. Only way a woman round here gets respect is by attaching herself to a man who's rich and powerful.'

'Like Spagsy Chiaparelli?'

'You hit it, doll.'

'But wouldn't it be jollissimo for you to gain people's respect apart from because of Spagsy?'

'What stuff you taking? That kinda thing don't happen.'

'My brother was really impressed by your singing.'

'Like I said, nice of him to say so.'

'He reckoned your voice could make you a big star . . .'

'Oh, sure,' said Choxy Mulligan sardonically.

'. . . not just a chanteuse in a speakeasy.'

'Listen up, buttercup. Spagsy's speakeasies are the only place I'm allowed to sing, and only when he's present. Even then he shoots any guy who smiles at me.'

'So, Choxy, do you actually *like* being a kept woman?'

'It sure as hell beats the alternative.'

Nobody can know how much further the two women might have advanced into the topic of women's rights, because at that moment Vic

'Rat Teeth' Papardelle and Michael 'Two Legs' Conchiglioni burst through the door. They stood either side, sentries for the entrance of Spagsy Chiaparelli.

And on his instructions, they took Twinks for a ride. What he called a 'can-can ride'.

*   *   *

Ziggy 'Tomato Sauce' Radiatore checked the piece of paper on which he'd written down the address: Sammy 'Broken Ankles' Lumache's garage on Broome Street.

He looked at his watch. Twenty-seven minutes past two in the afternoon. No chance the target would be there before four, but Ziggy 'Tomato Sauce' Radiatore always got everywhere in good time.

He once again checked the mechanism of his selected weapons. He had decided on his favourite Colt Vest Pocket Pistol. Small, neat and efficient. Two of them, though, both checked and primed. Though he'd never needed to use the second gun, he left nothing to chance. It was just as well Ziggy 'Tomato Sauce' Radiatore hadn't indulged the vanity of scratching notches on the pistols' butts; if he had, there wouldn't have been any butts left.

*   *   *

Blotto wished for Corky Froggett more than ever as he drove through the drab outskirts of New York City. The Lagonda just didn't feel right. Maybe the finely honed machine was simply expressing its disapproval of driving on the wrong side of the

177

road. But Blotto felt there was something even more serious going on. The car seemed to be experiencing a heartsickness that reflected his own.

As the Lagonda entered Manhattan, the buildings grew taller and, even if there had been much light, little of it would have penetrated down to street level. It was a cold, grey afternoon. The rain didn't blow about as much as in Chicago, but it was still thick and relentless.

The traffic in the city was heavy, a maelstrom of clogged buses, screeching taxicabs and screaming taxi drivers, as Blotto progressed slowly downtown. The directions Luther P. Chapstick III had given him were good, and he didn't have much difficulty in nosing his way towards his destination. Through the dense traffic he still didn't notice the small Chevrolet that had stayed some three or four vehicles behind him all the way from Chicago.

In the Lagonda's glove compartment lay a thick envelope, the purpose of his mission. He didn't know what was in it, and he didn't care. All Blotto knew was that once the envelope had been handed over to Harry 'Three Bananas' Pennoni in Sammy 'Broken Ankles' Lumache's garage, his job would be done. He'd then have to turn tail and retrace his melancholy steps back to Chapstick Towers and matrimony.

*   *   *

Ziggy 'Tomato Sauce' Radiatore had spoken to Sammy 'Broken Ankles' Lumache and persuaded him of the wisdom of taking a coffee break. The boss and his mechanics had obediently adjourned to a local trattoria for a couple of hours, leaving the

178

garage unattended.

Before they left, Radiatore had got them to shift some of the automobiles, so that there was now only one obvious bay into which any incoming vehicle could park. Then he'd taken up his position inside the doorway. Anyone who'd just driven as far as his quarry was bound to park in the only available space and then get out of the driver's seat and stand up to stretch his weary limbs.

It was then that Ziggy 'Tomato Sauce' Radiatore would add to his total by drilling a single shot neatly through the man's temples.

*   *   *

Blotto turned the Lagonda from Mulberry Street on to Broome Street. Unnoticed, the small Chevrolet did the same.

The sign for Sammy 'Broken Ankles' Lumache's garage was grubby but perfectly legible. The doorway's shutter was pulled up. A single light illuminated the interior.

Blotto swung the Lagonda inside to the only available space. He pushed against the steering wheel and felt the weariness in his limbs. It had been a long, long drive.

Then he opened the driver's door and stepped out, stretching as he did so.

At that moment a gunshot rang out. Blotto ducked.

Inwardly Ziggy 'Tomato Sauce' Radiatore cursed. He'd had the bead of his Colt trained on the spot where the car's driver must inevitably appear. And then the slimebag had got out of the passenger side of the vehicle! Damn, he'd have to use the second pistol, and doing that was a blow to his professional pride.

He moved swiftly forward. No risks this time. The Judas kill. Close enough to kiss the guy.

Ziggy 'Tomato Sauce' Radiatore looked into the bewildered cornflower-blue eyes of Blotto as he raised his Colt to his target's temple.

A shot rang out.

And Ziggy 'Tomato Sauce' Radiatore crumpled to the garage floor. Dead.

24

Some Explanations

In seconds Blotto had seized his faithful cricket bat from its front seat perch and held it ready to beat off any further assaults. The briefest of looks at the hired assassin at his feet told him no more would come from that direction.

But the corpulent young man with pebble glasses who was walking towards him from the haphazardly parked Chevrolet, carrying an Accrington-Murphy PL23 hunting rifle, might prove to be a great threat. With a quick feint to one side, Blotto moved towards the wavering gun barrel, dropped to one knee and with a fine upward stroke of his cricket bat, sent the rifle skittering across the garage floor.

One more smooth movement and his assailant was immobilized in a full nelson. 'Tell me, you lump of toadspawn,' demanded Blotto, 'who are you?'

'My name,' said the young man, 'will never be revealed—even under torture.'

They decided to leave the body (which they didn't know belonged to New York's finest hitman, Ziggy 'Tomato Sauce' Radiatore) on the garage floor. No doubt the New York police force had methods for dealing with that kind of thing.

Keeping the man who'd been tailing him covered with the Accrington-Murphy PL23 hunting rifle, Blotto dragooned his captive into the driving seat of the Lagonda. Still with the gun trained on him, the young man was ordered to drive a few blocks north of Little Italy and to park outside a chophouse his captor had noticed on the way down. 'I don't know about you, me old greengage,' said Blotto, who was just realizing how long it had been since his last meal, 'but I could eat a horse—snaffle, stirrups and saddle!'

The young man, who'd driven the same route and therefore suffered the same dietary deprivation, agreed that he too was extremely hungry.

'But listen,' said Blotto, 'I'm going to lock your Accrington-Murphy PL23 hunting rifle in the dickey. I'm assuming you're not carrying any other weapons . . .?'

'Not a thing, I promise.'

'Good ticket. Well, let's wrap the choppers round some chow, and then maybe you can give me a few explanations . . .?'

*   *   *

When he looked at his steak, for the first time Blotto appreciated the Americans' rather vulgar desire to have the biggest of everything. It not only overlapped its plate, it overlapped the table, while also providing a platform for piles of eggs, fried potatoes, onions and tomatoes, which required further covering with salt, pepper, thin American mustard and catsup. His perhaps unwilling companion had ordered the same. Both had beers. By unspoken consent they agreed not to talk until the bulk of their eating had been done.

Finally, as Blotto pushed his last bit of fried potato round his plate to soak up the remainder of the meaty juices, he turned to the man who'd trailed him all the way from Chicago and said: 'Perhaps I should be thanking you. You really saved my chitterlings there. That boddo you shot was out to coffinate me, you know.'

'Yes.' Then the man admitted, 'Actually, I didn't mean to hit him.'

'Oh?'

'No, I was aiming at you.'

'Ah.'

'I wanted to kill you.'

The social rules that had been ferociously inculcated into Blotto during his upbringing had not, so far as he could remember, covered the correct response to someone who's just announced they wanted to kill you. So he confined himself to a 'Toad-in-the-hole!'

'In fact, I still want to kill you,' insisted the chubbily earnest, bespectacled young man opposite him.

'Well, I'll be jugged like a hare!' said Blotto. 'Can I ask why?'

'Because,' the young man announced dramatically, 'you've been slipping the sweets to my girl.'

'I'm sorry? Are you telling me you're another "very close friend" of Choxy Mulligan?'

A puzzled wrinkle of the brow. 'I've never heard of anyone called Choxy Mulligan.'

There was a considerable congestion of pennies inside Blotto's brain, but this was an example of those rare occasions when one of them dropped. He remembered being with Twinks while she inspected a copse at Tawcester Towers. He remembered her description of Briscoe Daubeney-Vere's killer as a corpulent man, five foot seven in height, who wore a size six shoe. He looked down surreptitiously to his dining companion's footwear before asking, 'Your name isn't by any chance Sophocles Katzenjammer, is it?'

The young man considered his options for a moment and then admitted that it was indeed his name.

Blotto's mental processes were on an uncharacteristic roll. 'And you want to kill me because you think I've been cornswiggling Mary Chapstick?' he asked, proud of the new word he'd learnt.

'Sure, that's why I want to kill you. And don't worry, next time I get the opportunity, you'll be a goner.'

'So just rein in the roans for a moment ...' Within Blotto's brain rings of logic were linking up at an unprecedented rate. 'You followed Mary and her father to England. You came to Tawcester Towers. It was you who tried to shoot me on the balcony after Twinks's impromptu dance, and ended up killing that poor old greengage Briscoe Daubeney-Vere by mistake.' Another memory came to him. 'It was you who shot my bails off in the game of cricket!' Blotto's face grew stern and forbidding. 'You know, I can't really forgive you for that.'

'All right, I know shooting at people's immoral, but—'

'Nothing to do with morality. Tawcester Towers was within three runs of winning that game.' But the memory of sporting disappointment was quickly pushed to one side. 'And it was you who shot at me on the SS *His Majesty*!'

Sophocles Katzenjammer nodded that yes, indeed, it had been.

'But why, in the name of strawberries, did you never hit me?'

The would-be assassin hung an apologetic head. 'Because I'm a very bad shot. It's my poor eyesight.'

'Oh tough Gorgonzola,' said Blotto, empathizing. He imagined how deprived his own childhood would have been if he'd not been able to go out and entertain himself by shooting any number of wildfowl and small mammals whenever he felt like it. For a moment he'd forgotten that Sophocles Katzenjammer's avowed ambition was to murder him.

Then another puzzling thought came to him. 'Why haven't you tried to shoot me since I've been in the United States?'

'I just did. In Sammy 'Broken Ankles' Lumache's garage on Broome Street. But again I hit the wrong guy.'

'Oh yes. But why not before that?'

'Because you've been under the protection of

Luther P. Chapstick III. I don't know if you've heard, but between the Chapsticks and the Katzenjammers there's quite a lot of bad blood.'

'What, in their meat products, you mean?'

'I didn't mean "bad blood" literally. I mean there's like a vendetta between our two families. It came to a head when I fell in love with Mary. She was as much in love with me as I was with her. We wanted to spend our lives together. But holy cow, when our families found out about it, there was blood all over the walls. Mary and I were "star-crossed lovers" for sure, like in that Shakespeare play . . .'

'*Hamlet*,' Blotto suggested helpfully. It was the only title he could remember.

'Anyway, there was a big stink. Both sets of parents forbidding us from seeing each other. We thought we'd got round them. We'd made plans to elope to Florida, get married down there. Fixed a time to meet at Chicago Union Station. But somehow my father got wind of what was going on and the day I was meant to meet Mary he locked me in the cellar of our house. And I've never spoken to her since.'

He allowed a moment for a tear to well up in his eye. Dashing it away, he continued, 'Anyway, the result was, if I ever strayed anywhere on to Luther P. Chapstick III's premises, I'd have signed my own death warrant. That's why I couldn't shoot you back in Chicago.'

'Oh. Well, thanks for explaining.' The cogs in Blotto's brain creaked and whirred as a new thought took shape. 'But hold back the hounds a moment . . . You say you want to kill me because I've been slipping the sweets to Mary Chapstick . . .'

185

'Too right I do!'

'But what makes you think I really want to slip the sweets to her? Or cornswiggle her, come to that?'

'Well, that ain't too tough a question. All Chicago knows you're about to marry the popsie.'

'Yes, but all Chicago doesn't know whether I actually want to marry the popsie or not.'

'Who cares about that? You're her fiancé, her father's set up a big reception at the Chainey Hotel, ninety per cent of the Mafia's been invited. You're going to get spliced to her, whether you like it or not.'

'And that's why you want to kill me? Simply because I'm going to marry her.'

'Sounds like enough reason to me! I love that girl. If I can't have her, I can't bear the thought of anyone else having her. And if I get sent down for your murder, I don't care. Let 'em hang me, let 'em fry me! My life will be meaningless if I cannot have Mary Chapstick!'

A blissful smile crept over Blotto's angelic features. 'Do you know, Sophocles,' he said, 'I don't think our ambitions in this situation are as far apart as they might be.'

*   *   *

The atmosphere between them had changed considerably. It was now positively bonhomous. As they plotted Sophocles Katzenjammer's elopement with the woman he loved, Blotto felt anxieties slipping off him like the condensation from a chilled champagne bottle brought into a warm room.

The constant mentions of Mary Chapstick

186

reminded him that he had promised to call her as soon as he got to New York. When he mentioned this, Sophocles said excitedly, 'Why don't I call her? Give her the good news that we can now be together for ever!'

But Blotto demurred. Twinks's experience had told them that the very walls of Chapstick Towers had ears. For the moment they must maintain the illusion that his engagement was still on. When they got back to Chicago, they'd have plenty of time to work out the details of their plan and let Mary know about it. Also, though he didn't want to diminish the growing admiration Sophocles Katzenjammer had for him by mentioning the fact, a project of the kind they were envisaging would get nowhere unless Twinks's amazing brain was applied to it.

So when he got through to Mary Chapstick, he started with what he imagined to be appropriate sentiments for a young man addressing his beloved fiancée. 'Well ... er ... um ... well ... erm ... I was—'

But Mary cut across his maundering. 'Blotto,' she announced in a voice of high anxiety, 'Twinks has gone missing! The word on the street in Chicago is that Spagsy Chiaparelli has got her!'

25

Where's Twinks?

The Lagonda still wasn't running at its brilliant best, but in spite of the car's sluggishness, Blotto made very good time back to Chicago. Having finally accepted that the Englishman wasn't a real rival for his beloved's affections, Sophocles Katzenjammer announced magnanimously that he no longer had homicidal tendencies towards him. And he was profusely sorry for the four attempts he had made on the life of his perceived rival. Blotto accepted this apology with characteristic grace. It didn't do for gentlemen to get into lasting disagreements over little things like trying to kill each other. (If ancient history like that was allowed to rankle, no members of the British aristocracy would ever speak to each other.)

So, while Blotto drove without stopping to reach Chicago the following evening, Sophocles Katzenjammer travelled back at a more sedate pace in his Chevrolet.

The minute the Lagonda came to a halt in the drive of Chapstick Towers Blotto was out and rushing into the house to see Mary Chapstick. Her father, watching from his study, smiled fondly at this display of youthful emotion. His prospective son-in-law had hitherto seemed a bit reticent and British about displays of emotion towards his fiancée, but the trip to New York seemed to have changed all that.

It had also proved that the boy had his uses. He

had evaded the vigilance of the New York cops and presumably delivered the agreed payment to Harry 'Three Bananas' Pennoni. Luther P. Chapstick III could think of many future jobs for which his son-in-law's innocent, patrician manner could once again provide a useful front.

Mary Chapstick was very thrilled when Blotto came bursting into her bedroom in the middle of the evening. It was the kind of convention-defying, romantic gesture she had always hoped for in a fiancé.

She was slightly less thrilled to find that his only interest seemed to be the whereabouts of his sister. But, consoling herself with the thought that once they were married they would have an entire lifetime to concentrate on each other, she passed on the little information that she had about Twinks's disappearance.

The only solid fact that emerged was that his sister was known to have been seen a couple of days before in the company of a private investigator called Paul Sidney.

Clasping his fiancée's hands in gratitude (which Mary Chapstick serendipitously interpreted as a deeper emotion), Blotto rushed back to the Lagonda and set off for the address in Bay Street.

*　　　*　　　*

Previous experience of night-time Chicago made him lock the car before making his way up to Paul Sidney's grubby office. He found the private investigator slumped head-down across his desk.

His first thought, that Spagsy Chiaparelli's hoods had got there before him and eliminated the potential witness, was quickly negated by the smell of scotch, the empty bottle on the desk, and loud snoring. Slapping the private eye awake, Blotto demanded news of his sister.

Paul Sidney did not volunteer his part in her capture; nor did he allude to the fee he had negotiated for his contribution. He did, however, offer information, though again not for nothing. Blotto fortunately had a full wallet, having taken a lot for emergency expenses on his New York trip.

For the entire contents—just over 2,000 dollars—the White Knight of Bay Street told all he knew: that Twinks had been taken into the temporary custody of Choxy Mulligan.

Blotto didn't pause to consider. While Paul Sidney reached into a filing cabinet to produce another bottle of scotch which he prepared to empty, Blotto found in his pocket the scrap of paper he'd been given in Spagsy Chiaparelli's speakeasy. Without hesitation he picked up the telephone and asked the operator for Choxy Mulligan's number.

The smoky voice answered and was not pleased to hear who was calling. She'd had a bellyful of being done wrong by men. She still resented the way Blotto had treated her and was not prepared to be cooperative. But when she heard that he was looking for his sister, Choxy's tone changed. Since Twinks's abduction she'd thought a lot about their conversation, about the rights of women, about how there might be other ways of getting through life that didn't involve seeking the protection of a strong male. Twinks's words had stirred some long-dormant assertiveness in Choxy Mulligan, and she would now do anything to help her new-found female friend.

Sadly, though, she thought in this instance any kind of help might come too late. 'Spagsy told Rat Teeth and Two Legs to take her for a ride.'

'What does that mean?'

'It means, I'm afraid, you should start making funeral arrangements. Though I figure it won't be one of those funerals where you find any filling for the coffin.'

'Some stenchers tried to take me for a ride,' Blotto recalled, 'but I don't think they succeeded. What actually does it mean when someone's "taken for a ride"?'

There was a pessimistic sigh from the other end of the phone. 'Can mean a lotta things. But in this case Spagsy specified that Twinks was to be taken on a "can-can ride".'

'Oh, I know about the can-can,' said Blotto eagerly, remembering a rather bizarre evening spent in Paris with Corky Froggett. 'It's a French dance.'

'Not such a cheery dance in this case,' said Choxy Mulligan gloomily. 'It involves taking the victim down to Chapstick's factory and by the end of the process ... well, Twinks probably didn't start out with a moo, but if she did, that's all that'd be left ...'

Blotto seemed perplexed, so she went on, 'It's a method Spagsy uses when he really wants to be sure of removing someone without trace. He says it's the ultimate form of democracy. Everybody in America stands a chance of getting a little bit of anybody.'

'In a can-can?' asked Blotto, still confused.

'Well, in a can, anyway,' said Choxy Mulligan.

It took a moment for Blotto's slow mind to

process the information that he was being given. But when it did get through, it hit with the impact of a St Louis Steamhammer.

'Great Wilberforce, no!' he cried, dropping the telephone on the desk of the once-again-insensible Paul Sidney. 'I must get to the Chapstick Manufacturing Plant to save Twinks!'

26

Taken for a Can-Can Ride

Running sluggishly or not, the Lagonda still tore up the ground between Bay Street and the Chapstick Manufacturing Plant. Though it was late evening and dark, none of the workers inside would have known it. Regardless of daylight and seasons they worked on, shift by shift, in their eternal cycle of slaughter. Nothing must be allowed to stop the accumulation of the Chapstick millions.

Remembering the geography from his guided tour, Blotto parked the Lagonda where Luther P. Chapstick III's car had been parked and, pausing only to gather up his trusty cricket bat, rushed into the building. Anyone who questioned where he was going received the steely stare with which Lyminsters had faced down the French at Crécy and was told that he was shortly to marry their boss's daughter. No one stood in his way.

As he rushed through the stockyards, mud and blood spattering up over the crumpled clothes in which he'd driven to New York and back, Blotto realized how safe Spagsy Chiaparelli's method

192

of disposing of people in this vast complex was. Whatever criminal activity they saw, none of the workers would ever tell anyone. They didn't want trouble, they wanted to hang on to their jobs. And besides, most of them were so mesmerized by the monotony of their work that they didn't notice anything that went on outside it.

Reminding himself of the sequence of processing rooms he had been shown through, Blotto tried to work out where Twinks was most likely to have been taken. He remembered the men with the sledgehammers abstractedly braining the cattle as they came past. Surely their huge implements would not be used to crush such a tiny nut as Twinks's cranium?

Then there were the workers who grabbed the stunned carcasses and chained them up on the hooks of the great wheel. Surely there was no need to do that with as slight a frame as his sister's?

Increasingly, as he rushed from room to room and saw no sign of her, all of his fears focused on one thing: The Great Grinder. He remembered the terrible crunching noise that had emanated from its vast maw and tried to keep out of his mind the image of Twinks's fragile form caught up in those fearsome cogs. He couldn't bear the thought of his precious sister being, as Luther P. Chapstick III had put it, 'spread on toast at breakfast tables all over the US of A'.

Blotto had been right. It was in the room of The Great Grinder that he found them. He could see the huge pinstriped frames of Vic 'Rat Teeth' Papardelle and Michael 'Two Legs' Conchiglioni and between them the slender form of Twinks, clad in *eau de nil* silk and struggling literally for

193

her life as she was forced inexorably over the blood-enslimed floor towards two ladders which led up to the gaping mouth of The Great Grinder.

With a cry of 'Put my sister down, you running sores!' Blotto leapt forward, brandishing the cricket bat, carrying which he had won the Eton and Harrow match almost single-handedly.

Vic 'Rat Teeth' Papardelle turned at the sound and was rewarded by a smash from the bat straight in his face. Had he had any more nose left to break, it would have been broken. The blow was sufficient momentarily to disorient him and loosen his grip on Twinks's arm as he floundered in the offal on the floor.

But the distraction only made Michael 'Two Legs' Conchiglioni bolder. Lifting the girl up bodily, he wrapped her around his shoulders like a scarf and started climbing one of the ladders towards The Great Grinder.

Blotto leapt towards him, but felt his ankle gripped by the steel fingers of Vic 'Rat Teeth' Papardelle. He brought the cricket bat down with a crunching blow on to the man's wrist and the grasp loosened.

But he had lost valuable seconds. When he looked back, Michael 'Two Legs' Conchiglioni was at the top of his ladder and Twinks was actually in mid-air, having been thrown into the devouring maw. Blotto shot up the ladder, brought the bat down with devastating force on to the middle of Michael 'Two Legs' Conchiglioni's fedora, then, as the man crashed to the floor, used his back as a springboard to fly on to the lip of the grinder and grab his sister's flailing hand.

He was only just in time. When he caught her,

one of her elegantly shod feet was inches from the whirring cogs, which spat out flying tendrils of entrails as they crushed the rest.

And their security was only relative. The rim of the huge funnel on which Blotto had landed was slick with blood and guts and even Twinks's sylphlike weight made his foothold more precarious. But he did manage to pull her up to balance on the lip beside him.

When, however, they looked down towards what they hoped was safety, they saw that Spagsy Chiaparelli's two heavies had found large implements shaped like boathooks with which they were approaching to topple them from their slippery stance. Vic 'Rat Teeth' Papardelle was climbing up one of the ladders, Michael 'Two Legs' Conchiglioni the other.

As he had so many times before, Blotto looked into his sister's azure eyes, knowing that somehow she would see a way out of their predicament.

'Larksissimo!' she cried. 'We can get out of this one, Blotto me old rhubarb crumble!' She made some quick calculations, looked upwards, pulled a length of fine silk out of her reticule and threw it up, so that the hook on its end caught in a giant blood-splattered ring on the room's ceiling.

'Hold tight on to me, Blotters! Use our weight to get the backswing, then put into action the Double Drumski we used to practise from the battlements of Tawcester Towers!'

'Tickey-tockey, Twinks me old pincushion!' cried her brother.

Like circus acrobats, the siblings clasped each other and launched themselves into the void above the churning entrails. Their impetus swung them almost to the back wall. By the time they returned, Vic 'Rat Teeth' Papardelle and Michael 'Two Legs' Conchiglioni were standing at the top of their respective ladders. Seeing the two Lyminsters hurtling towards them and not having time to bring their boathooks into play, the heavies took evasive action and the pair sailed neatly between them. On the return swing Blotto and Twinks each put out a practised leg at the relevant moment. Blotto's caught Vic 'Rat Teeth' Papardelle in the small of the back and toppled him neatly into The Great Grinder, while Twinks's did the same service for Michael 'Two Legs' Conchiglioni.

'That,' said Twinks with satisfaction, 'was pure creamy éclair.'

'Yes,' her brother agreed. 'You absolutely are the nun's nightie.'

She laughed off the compliment and slapped her rather dirty hands together. 'I don't think we'll see a lot more of those two.'

'No,' said Blotto with a slight giggle. 'Soon they'll be spread on toast at breakfast tables all over the US of A.'

27

Playing Cupid

It was Twinks's view (sensible as ever) that they weren't safe on the streets of Chicago. Between them Spagsy Chiaparelli and Luther P. Chapstick III owned the town. The news of Vic 'Rat Teeth' Papardelle and Michael 'Two Legs'

Conchiglioni's fate must reach their ears soon. Chiaparelli, who didn't like failure, would then charge more of his gang members with the task of finding and eliminating Twinks. And there was no way Chapstick would let her brother escape his impending wedding.

As they sat in the Lagonda a few streets away from the Chapstick Manufacturing Plant and pondered these matters, Blotto told his sister briefly about his encounter with Sophocles Katzenjammer.

'Well, that's jollissimo, Blotters,' she cried. 'He still loves Mary, does he?'

'Toad-in-the-hole, yes! He thinks she's the absolute crystallized ginger.'

'So all we have to do is to arrange for them to meet up again and elope. Then we're out of the undergrowth and we'll be rolling on camomile lawns!'

'But where's going to be safe for us to meet him?' asked Blotto.

His sister looked at her blood- and offal-stained *eau de nil* dress. 'And, more important, at least as far as I'm concerned, where are we going to get a change of clothes?'

Blotto looked at his watch. It was still the small hours of the morning. 'None of the big stores'll be open yet.'

'Great whiffling water rats, Blotto! We can't just walk into Marshall Field's on State Street looking like scrapings from a butcher's floor. Spagsy Chiaparelli'd know about it in no time. Hmm ... Do we have any friends in this murdey city?'

'Wasn't there some incorruptible private investigator you said you'd had dealings with?'

Twinks grimaced. 'Forget him. He turned out to

be as corrupt as a five-year-old Stilton.'

Blotto began cautiously, 'Well, I think Sophocles Katzenjammer is now on my side . . . even though he tried to kill me.'

'Might be risky. We know the Katzenjammers are at daggers drawn with the Chapsticks, but they may still be in the pockets of Spagsy Chiaparelli.' Twinks's fine forehead wrinkled as she brought her brain to bear on the problem. In a matter of seconds it cleared and she cried out, 'Choxy Mulligan!'

'But contacting her was the trigger for all the fumacious stuff that's happened since,' her brother objected.

'Yes, but I've talked to Choxy woman to woman.'

Blotto was silent. Having been brought up—or rather neglected—throughout his childhood by the Dowager Duchess, he knew how powerful a woman could be. And when you'd got two of the creatures together—'woman to woman'—well, it was clearly time for chaps to stay mum on the sidelines.

Following Twinks's instruction, he drove the Lagonda until they found an outdoor payphone booth. Needless to say, his sister did the talking.

He looked up hopefully as she emerged from the booth. 'Choxy's got a safe place. I knew she would have. Gloria's Hairdressing and Manicure Salon on Dicker Street. She says it's one venue she knows Spagsy Chiaparelli would never go to. Apparently he likes dames to look purty, but how they get to look purty he doesn't want to know. We're to be there at seven thirty.' She looked at her tiny silver wristwatch. 'Less than two hours.'

Blotto drove the Lagonda to Dicker Street and, following the instructions given by Choxy, parked out of sight in a garage round the back of the hairdresser's. There they waited till the black of the sky was cracked by slivers of dawn light.

Then, on the dot of half past seven, again as instructed by Choxy, they tapped on the metal door at the back of the garage. They were expected. One of Gloria's stylists, dressed in a crisp white tunic, let them in and led them to a small room at the back of the salon. She passed no comment on their offal-stained clothes, but offered them coffee, which they gratefully accepted.

Within minutes, Choxy Mulligan was with them. Blotto was amazed, given that the two women had spent only a very brief time together—and not in the most tranquil of circumstances—how relaxed they seemed together.

The chanteuse had a suitcase with her. She opened it to reveal a tweed suit and accoutrements for Blotto; and for Twinks, a choice of six dresses. 'I know we girls can get picky about what we wear.'

Twinks selected a creation in deep maroon. Different from her usual pale colours, but she knew she could carry it off.

Choxy Mulligan showed them the way to the salon's bathrooms, where they showered and changed into the clothes provided. Both felt considerably more themselves when they no longer smelt of cows' entrails.

Then they rejoined Choxy. Quickly they outlined their plans to get Mary Chapstick and Sophocles Katzenjammer back together and asked for any advice on how that could be achieved. The singer proved as resourceful as Twinks. She said that, though for safety reasons he hid it from Spagsy Chiaparelli, Luther P. Chapstick III secretly had the hots for her. He'd do anything that might ingratiate him with her.

So she called Chapstick Towers and announced to the owner that she knew the perfect hairdressing salon to send a stylist to do his daughter's hair 'on the big day'. Predictably enough, Luther P. Chapstick III thought this was a dandy idea, and arranged an eleven o'clock appointment that morning for Mary to discuss her requirements.

Then it was Blotto's turn to ring Sophocles Katzenjammer, who had been eagerly awaiting his call. The young man promised to be with them in as little time as it took.

Then Twinks and Choxy Mulligan started busying themselves with wedding plans. Blotto, blissfully secure in the knowledge that it wasn't his wedding they were planning, sat and read the newspaper's sports pages. He didn't understand a word, but there was a kind of perverse enjoyment in seeing how excited these Yanks could get about rounders.

Sophocles Katzenjammer arrived in paroxysms of excitement. His chubby cheeks wobbled, his poppy eyes bobbled behind their thick glasses. He couldn't believe that soon he would be in the company of the beloved one whom he had so often despaired of ever seeing again.

The two women joined the men for a council of strategy. 'It's important, Sophocles,' said Twinks, 'that you and Mary get married as soon as possible, before either of your parents get wind of what's going on.'

'Before Spagsy gets to hear about it too,' interposed Choxy. 'He likes playing Chapstick off against the Katzenjammers. He ain't gonna like anything that might lead to a reconciliation between the two families.'

'I don't think that's a very likely prospect,' said Sophocles Katzenjammer. 'The vendetta between them is as bad as ever—and I think it's about to get worse.'

'Oh?' asked Twinks.

'Let's just say that some information came to my father about a devious plot Chapstick was hatching to ruin our business. Goodness knows where it came from.'

Twinks smiled serenely. She knew where it came from.

'Anyway,' the young man went on, 'that gave my father the idea of getting ahead of the game and playing the same dirty trick on Chapstick. I don't think relations between the two families will improve when the offal from that little scheme hits the fan.'

'All the more reason to get you married off as soon as possible,' advised Choxy Mulligan.

'Tickey-tockey,' Twinks agreed.

Sophocles Katzenjammer looked a little shamefaced. 'It's a great idea, but I wish I could feel certain that Mary still loves me . . .'

'Of course she does!' said Blotto rather forcibly. Everything was going so well. He didn't want to see the project derailed by the fickle emotions of a mere girl.

'But she's been engaged to you, Blotto, and Mary is a creature of honour. That's one of the reasons why I love her so much. She might not want to break her engagement to you.'

'Oh, don't talk such toffee. Of course she will.'

'But there's you, tall, strong, incredibly

handsome—and an English aristocrat, to boot. And there's me—small, ineffectual, short-sighted—and son of her father's mortal enemy. Why on earth should she choose me?'

'She should choose you,' Blotto replied with some force, 'because, by Denzil, I do not want to spend the rest of my life driving on the wrong side of the road, saying "gotten" when it should be "got" and watching rounders!'

It was agreed—much to Blotto's dismay—that when Mary Chapstick arrived at eleven, the engaged couple should have a brief tête-à-tête before Sophocles Katzenjammer was introduced into the equation.

Miserably, Blotto returned to the rounders scores, while Twinks and Choxy—with occasional interruptions from Sophocles Katzenjammer—continued their wedding planning.

*   *   *

One of the Chapstick Towers limousines deposited Mary Chapstick at the door of Gloria's Hairdressing and Manicure Salon on the dot of eleven o'clock. To her surprise the stylist with whom she had the appointment led her to a back room. Surprise turned to elation when she discovered that its only occupant was Blotto.

As soon as they were alone, she threw her arms around his neck with a cry of 'My love! Seeing you makes my life complete!'

Broken biscuits, thought Blotto. This isn't getting off to a very good start.

But he had to persevere. Relying on the very hasty training that Twinks and Choxy had just given him, he said, 'How I wish that were true.'

His fiancée was taken aback. 'What can you mean, Blotto?'

'I mean that sadly I cannot make your life complete.'

'Yes, you can,' she assured him, with the certainty of a child who had always got her own way.

'No. You may think you love me, but there will always be one whom you love more than me.'

'What garbage you're talking, Blotto.'

'Listen to me, you poor pineapple. I am not the first man whom you've thought you wanted to marry.'

'That was a long time ago. Besides, he did something unforgivable. He stood me up!'

'Ah, but there was a reason why he stood you up!'

'No reason is sufficient to explain standing a woman up at Chicago Union Station!' announced Mary Chapstick, once again sounding unnervingly like her father. 'The sense of humiliation can never be completely eradicated.'

'Not even,' suggested Blotto, 'if the young man you were meant to meet had been locked in a cellar that day by his scheming father . . .?'

'Surely that didn't . . .' Blotto's words had struck home, but she still wasn't totally convinced. 'Where do you get this information from?'

'From the boddo himself—none other than Sophocles Katzenjammer.'

Her face went pale. 'You have seen Sophocles Katzenjammer?'

'Very recently. I was in a chophouse in New York with him only a couple of days ago . . .'

'Oh . . .'

'And, Mary, he still loves you as much as ever.'

Another 'Oh . . .' Then a tear glinted in her dark eye. 'But even if he does, our love cannot be!'

'Why not, for the love of strawberries?'

'Because I am betrothed to another!'

'Only me, though.'

'Blotto, in the time we have known each other, my respect for you has increased on a daily basis. You are a fine, honourable man—and who cares if you are as dim as a one-dime candle?'

'Oh, thank you,' said Blotto.

'But I could not compromise the respect I have for you by abandoning you. You love me. We are engaged to be married. I am not such an unprincipled woman as to betray such an agreement. I will go through with the marriage!'

In his briefing session with Twinks and Choxy, Blotto had been dissuaded from his intention to say at this point, 'Hoopee-doopee! Then we need never clap our peepers on each other again!' The two women suggested kindly that in such circumstances people of their gender preferred to be let down a little more gently.

So, using the words that they had taught him, Blotto instead said, 'You are very honourable, Mary. And losing you will leave an icy void at the centre of my heart for ever. But marriage can only work if there's equal love on both sides. If I twiddle the reef-knot with you, Mary, I'll be condemning you to a life of unhappiness.'

'How can you say that?'

'Because it is true,' asserted Blotto. 'You would do the honourable thing and marry me, because that is the kind of fine, upstanding girl you are.

But throughout your life you would know that the person you were really still in love with was Sophocles Katzenjammer.' The girl was silent. 'Come on, you cannot deny that is true. Can you, Mary?'

Tears ran down her cheeks as a very small 'No' emerged from her full lips.

'Then let's light the fireworks of fun!' cried Blotto. 'I can now reveal to you that Sophocles Katzenjammer is actually in this building as we speak.'

'What?' A rich glow suffused the beautiful cheeks of Mary Chapstick.

'And it will be a matter of moments for me to introduce him to you.'

'Oh, Blotto,' said Mary, as he rushed to the door. 'There's just one thing I want to say . . .'

'Well, shift your shimmy. Young love can't wait, you know.'

'I just want to say, Blotto, that you are the most selfless and honourable man I have ever met.'

He blushed boyishly and mumbled, 'Oh, don't talk such toffee.'

*   *   *

The rest of the morning was busy, but extremely satisfactory. As soon as Sophocles Katzenjammer and Mary Chapstick met, they fell into each other's arms. No one witnessing their reunion could be in any doubt that what they shared was The Real Thing.

Twinks and Choxy's wedding planning had paid off in spades. They had the special licence by eleven thirty. By twelve the young couple were in a little chapel Choxy Mulligan knew. By twelve thirty they had been married by a partially unfrocked minister who, as Choxy reminded him, owed a favour to Spagsy Chiaparelli. The service was witnessed by Choxy Mulligan and the stylist from Gloria's. Twinks acted as bridesmaid and Blotto was the best man.

By one fifteen Mr and Mrs Sophocles Katzenjammer were on a train puffing out of Chicago Union Station on the way to start their married life in Florida.

*   *   *

Blotto and Twinks said fond farewells to Choxy Mulligan and returned in high glee to Gloria's Hairdressing and Manicure Salon. All they wanted to do was leap into the Lagonda, drive down to New York and catch the first available liner back to England and Tawcester Towers.

But the day did hold one more surprise for them. Because they'd left some of their belongings inside, they went through the front entrance to the salon. And there they saw, being expensively primped and powdered, the Dowager Duchess of Framlington, a.k.a. Harvey the Tawcester Towers housemaid.

Their polite enquiries after her welfare produced a torrent of misery. Though generous, Luther P. Chapstick III, it appeared, was not someone who improved on acquaintance. He kept her as a virtual prisoner in the Chainey Hotel and she was sick of masquerading as a dowager duchess. She was feeling very homesick for Tawcester Towers—and she was even sicker of being in a country where everyone drove on the wrong side of the road.

It was a matter of moments for Blotto and Twinks to agree to take her back in the Lagonda with them. But they did point out that on the liner she'd have to stop this Dowager Duchess of Framlington nonsense and travel steerage.

28

The Fall of an Empire

The news of his daughter's eloping and his mistress's absconding did not improve the already sour mood of Luther P. Chapstick III. And the fact that his precious Mary-Bob was now the wife of a Katzenjammer only rubbed salt in the wound.

He was getting grief on other fronts too. Threatening calls from Harry 'Three Bananas' Pennoni asserting that he'd never received the promised bullion payment made Chapstick suspicious. Was the New York *capo dei capi* trying to swindle him? Or was he part of a conspiracy with Spagsy Chiaparelli? The Chicago Boss denied that he'd appropriated the bullion, but Luther P. Chapstick III found himself trusting the man less and less. He felt like a dupe and it was not a role that he relished.

Mind you, Spagsy Chiaparelli wasn't very cheerful either. Not only had he somehow lost two of his most reliable operatives, Vic 'Rat Teeth' Papardelle and Michael 'Two Legs' Conchiglioni, Choxy Mulligan was starting to get antsy with him. Confident that he wanted her too much actually to have her iced, the chanteuse had moved out of the apartment he paid for and bought her own place, to which she allowed him diminishing access. She had also got herself a manager who promised to lift her singing career out of the speakeasies and on to Broadway and Hollywood.

In another development Spagsy Chiaparelli could not understand, Choxy Mulligan also announced that at some point she wanted to do a college degree course. Since, so far as she could ascertain, an academic discipline called 'Women's Studies' did not yet exist, Choxy was determined to start one.

(She subsequently published a book, *From Speakeasy to Self-Respect*, which made little impact at the time, but was later reissued and revered as a seminal text by 1960s feminists.)

Then to add to Spagsy's woes, there were strong rumours around that the US government was shortly to end Prohibition.

Increasingly, he spent his time drinking, eating pasta with curiously nicknamed henchmen, fingering his scar and regretting the good old days.

What caused the final comeuppance of Luther P. Chapstick III was being hoist with his own petard. Copies of the documents from his desk that Twinks had photographed she had had sent to the Katzenjammer family. Sophocles' father, recognizing a good idea when he saw one, immediately set in motion Luther's plan in reverse, infiltrating workers into the Chapstick Manufacturing Plant. After a few months, at a given signal, they started mixing poison into the entire range of Chapstick products.

The results were predictably catastrophic. The national distribution of Chapstick's Canned Beef,

Chapstick's Corned Beef, Chapstick's Dressed Beef, Chapstick's Beef Sausages—not to mention Chapstick's specially flavoured Beef Extract—was such that no state escaped the mass poisoning.

Luther P. Chapstick III responded by paying millions of dollars to professionals in the developing field of public relations. But no amount of money can erase the memories of that much vomiting and diarrhoea. Chapstick beef products never regained their reputation or their hold on the market. People who still wanted to buy Beef Extract went for the Katzenjammer version. Chapstick Towers was sold and its owner declared bankrupt.

Meanwhile down in Florida the blissfully happy Mr and Mrs Sophocles Katzenjammer, without subsidy from either of their families, became pioneers in what would later be called 'organic farming' and nurtured their ever-growing brood of small vegetarians.

29

Another Summons to the Blue Morning Room

To say that Blotto and Twinks were welcomed back to Tawcester Towers with open arms would never have been accurate. The arms of the Dowager Duchess had done many things in their time, chiefly holding horses' reins, dogs' leads and guns, but they had never been sullied by hugging her children.

However, the siblings' late November return

from the United States of America that year was greeted with a distinct frost. The house itself was frosty, because its antiquated central heating system was still not functioning. But the frost that emanated from the Dowager Duchess was even more severe. So far as she was concerned, Blotto had failed to salvage the family honour. He had been sent to Chicago expressly to marry Mary Chapstick and thus refinance Tawcester Towers and he had not fulfilled that obligation. The Dowager Duchess was *very disappointed.*

The inevitable summons came the morning after their late-night arrival at Tawcester Towers. Blotto was down at the garage, describing and seeking expert explanations from Corky Froggett for the sluggish running of his Lagonda when one of the footmen told him that the Dowager Duchess required his immediate presence in the Blue Morning Room.

This was of course ominous, so asking Corky to check out everything on the car, Blotto had immediately obeyed his mother's summons. When he arrived at the place his mother regarded as her private court of law, Blotto found a very subdued Twinks was already there.

'I am *severely disappointed* in both of you,' the Dowager Duchess announced from her Chippendale throne, 'but more particularly in you, Blotto.'

Her son hung his blond-thatched head.

'My instructions were perfectly clear. Your engagement to Mary Chapstick was arranged between her father and myself before you had even left this country. I am at a loss to imagine what might have caused you to break it.'

Blotto considered a few responses. Saying that they'd found Luther P. Chapstick III to be a thumping crook wouldn't wash. And saying that Mary Chapstick was now married to the only man she truly loved would also go down like cocoa skin. So he remained silent, allowing his mother to continue.

Which of course she did. 'Your behaviour demonstrates a selfishness that I had hoped never to witness from a member of the Lyminster family. You were fully aware of the financial need that had made me decide on the undesirable course of marrying you off to an American, and yet you thought nothing of sabotaging my carefully conceived plans. You have placed me in a dilemma from which I cannot see an immediate way out. I fear I may be forced to disown you unless you can—'

'Oh, but Mater, you can't disown Blotto. He'll—'

'Silence, Twinks!' boomed the Dowager Duchess, fixing her Gorgon stare on her daughter before turning it back on her son. 'So, Blotto, can you provide me with any reason why I should not disown you?'

'Well ... er ... um ...'

'Unless you can provide some other way of refilling the Tawcester Towers coffers, you leave me with little alternative. So do you have a solution to offer?'

'Well ... er ... um ... I suppose I could try getting a job ... -?'

'I'm being serious, Blotto, so I will thank you not to indulge in feeble witticisms.'

'Well ... er ... um ... I suppose I ...' But nothing came. Blotto was in a real gluepot, a gluepot to make all previous gluepots look as minor as hangnails. As he had done before *in extremis*, he contemplated prayer. Being Church of England, he didn't really possess anything that could be counted as faith, but you never knew for sure, it might be worth trying ... So he prayed to someone or something to extricate him from his current mess.

His prayer was answered by a discreet tap on the Blue Morning Room door.

'Come!' barked the Dowager Duchess.

The door opened to admit a very deferential Corky Froggett, hiding something behind the peaked cap in his hand.

'Can you explain,' demanded the Dowager Duchess furiously, 'what could possibly justify the irruption of a mere chauffeur into this part of the house?'

'I apologize, Your Grace,' said Corky Froggett humbly, 'but what I have discovered will, I hope, explain my gross breach of decorum.'

'What is it?' came the testy reply.

'This!' Dramatically, the chauffeur moved his hat and lifted up in the other hand an ingot of gold. Blotto couldn't read it at that distance, but he knew that on the bar would be printed the words: 'PROPERTY OF U.S. GOVERNMENT'.

Corky Froggett addressed him. 'This, milord, is the explanation for the Lagonda's slow performance. A special compartment had been attached to the underside of the Lagonda's chassis. It was full of bars like this.'

The Dowager Duchess turned her eyes on her younger son. Her face was contorted into the nearest it could approximate to a beam.

'So, Blotto, are you telling me that you actually

came up with a plan to solve the Tawcester Towers financial crisis?'

It wasn't in his nature to lie, but on this occasion, emboldened by the look he saw in his sister's eye, Blotto replied, 'Yes, I weighed up the alternative appeals of getting money by marriage and getting it in a more tangible form. I always think gold's a safe investment in a crisis, don't you, Mater?'

The Dowager Duchess agreed and ordered Corky Froggett to bring the rest of the bullion into the Blue Morning Room as soon as possible.

It was then that Twinks said, 'But are you sure we have the right to keep it, Mater? Given that every bar is printed with the words: "PROPERTY OF U.S. GOVERNMENT" . . .?'

The Dowager Duchess of Tawcester, proud inheritor of the values that had kept the British aristocracy for so long at the top of the pile, looked at her daughter in amazement. 'Don't be so ridiculous, you silly chit!' she said. 'We'll scrape that off.'

*   *   *

So life returned to normal at Tawcester Towers. The plumbing was replaced in double quick time, with the result that by Christmas some areas of the house were almost warm. And restoration work was started on the damaged dukes in the Long Gallery.

A somewhat shamefaced Harvey returned to her duties and to Grimshaw. He said she deserved to be severely punished for what she'd done in the States. So they both enjoyed that.

Twinks, rather at a loose end, finished her

translation of Montaigne's *Essais* into Japanese and then, for fun, translated her Japanese version into Serbo-Croat.

And Blotto . . .? Hardly worth asking the question, really. He lovingly reacquainted himself with Mephistopheles, and the pair of them went off hunting.